Kinzua

Also by William N. Hoover

GRASS FLATS

Kinzua

From Cornplanter to the Corps

William N. Hoover

iUniverse, Inc.
New York Lincoln Shanghai

Kinzua
From Cornplanter to the Corps

Copyright © 2004, 2006 by William N. Hoover

iUniverse books may be ordered through booksellers or by contacting:

iUniverse
2021 Pine Lake Road, Suite 100
Lincoln, NE 68512
www.iuniverse.com
1-800-Authors (1-800-288-4677)

ISBN-13: 978-0-595-38116-6 (pbk)
ISBN-13: 978-0-595-82487-8 (cloth)
ISBN-13: 978-0-595-82483-0 (ebk)
ISBN-10: 0-595-38116-2 (pbk)
ISBN-10: 0-595-82487-0 (cloth)
ISBN-10: 0-595-82483-8 (ebk)

Printed in the United States of America

~ for Rhonda

ACKNOWLEDGEMENTS

First and foremost—I am indebted to the Warren County Historical Society (WCHS) for access to their extensive archives, for the professional manuscript editing and assistance provided by the Executive Director/Editor, Rhonda J. Hoover. I am also grateful to the WCHS Board of Directors for permission to publish the historical images found within this book.

I am obliged to the photographers who meticulously recorded the changing landscape of these ancient Allegheny hills and their namesake river during the years of construction of the Kinzua Dam. Of particular note is Mr. Everett Stoke, a professional photographer for more than a half-century. A great deal of his photographic documentation of Kinzua was created as irreplaceable aerial images. Many image archives have been explored and research reveals that these images will be seen here for the first time in nearly a half-century—some for the first time ever.

Research has drawn at length upon the works of Warren County historians: Merle H. Deardorff and Ernest C. Miller. The papers of Harold C. Putnam also presented invaluable historical details, particularly rich and abundant lore regarding the lives of Allegheny rivermen and the lumber rafts they piloted.

A debt is acknowledged to the work of all the news reporters and the papers for which they worked; these include *Warren Times Mirror, Warren Times Observer, Bradford Era, Bradford Journal, Youngstown Vindicator, Erie Sunday Times-Mirror, Erie Sunday Times-News, Buffalo Evening News, Pittsburgh Sun-Telegraph, Greater Pittsburgh Magazine, Pittsburgh Post-Gazette,* and *New York Times.*

I am appreciative of the Warren Library Association's assistance in delivering this manuscript to the publisher. Their T-1 connection made submission via the Internet quick and painless.

Personal notes, scrapbooks, news clippings and interviews contributed to the story, as individuals and families documented the innumerable changes experienced and endured during construction of the Kinzua Dam and Allegheny Reservoir. Some tirelessly followed the evolving development of the dam over the decades. Exceptional individuals meticulously maintained their own documentation. Of particular note is Joseph Wick of North Warren, Pennsylvania, who for thirty years created oversized scrapbooks which total 1,486 pages; including 839 snapshots, 1,337 news clippings, and copious correspondence for a grand total of 4,324 items from 164 separate sources. Such was the immense interest in Kinzua Dam. The efforts of these individuals allow the year-to-year transformations in the social, political, and geographic environments to be seen from a unique perspective and with a keen eye.

AUTHOR'S NOTE

Allegheny is a frequently occurring word in *Kinzua*—it refers to a river, a reservoir, a reservation, the hills, the mountains, a national forest, and also a state park. There are various spellings, but for *Kinzua* two specific spellings are used: Allegheny and Allegany. Both spellings are correct, but generally *Allegheny* is used in Pennsylvania and *Allegany* is used in New York. No need to explore the etymology, just a brief note for clarification, as both spellings may be found on a page or within a single paragraph in *Kinzua—from Cornplanter to the Corps*.

The cover image is a composite of Kinzua Dam and Solomon O'Bail, grandson of Cornplanter. Solomon O'Bail was selected because the duration of his life best represents the time span covered by *Kinzua*. For example, mid-way between the birth of his grandfather, Cornplanter, and the dedication of Kinzua Dam, Solomon O'Bail petitioned the Pennsylvania legislature to have a monument erected to commemorate his grandfather. This monument, the first ever erected to honor an Indian Chief, was dedicated on the original Cornplanter Grant in 1866—precisely one hundred years before the dedication of the completed Kinzua Dam.

The image and map list includes credit to the original photographer or specific historical collection, whenever this could be determined. If the photographer could not be identified then credit is given to Warren County Historical Society (WCHS), as all images are part of their varied and extensive archives. If any photographer was overlooked, it is regrettable, as every effort was made to identify the originator of each image. Maps were created by the author. They were derived and produced as a composite of many other maps, both old and new, to best represent the era.

The lyrics of the protest song *As Long as the Grass Shall Grow* are from the 1964 Johnny Cash *Bitter Tears* recording. Peter LaFarge, Indian friend of Cash, wrote the protest song.

To write a history that chronicles more than two centuries, I have admittedly taken minor liberties with time. At certain points I have compressed it, so the story may better be told.

~ wnh

CONTENTS

Image and Map List

Timeline

A savage place—as lonely and enchanted
As e'er beneath a waning moon was haunted.

~ W.J. McKnight

Historical Timeline:

1722

- The Tuscarora Indians, refugees from North Carolina, became the sixth member of the Iroquois Confederacy, under the sponsorship of the Oneida Indians.

1750

- Cornplanter was born around this date near what is now present-day Avon, New York. His mother was a Seneca of the Wolf Clan. Cornplanter's father was John O'Bail (Abeel), a white man from a prominent Dutch family.

1777

- July 1, Oswego, the Seneca decided to side with the British in the colonial struggle for independence. By daring acts of courage and leadership, Cornplanter emerged as a principle War Chief in the Iroquois Confederacy.

1779

- Revolutionary War generals, Sullivan and Clinton, campaigned against the Iroquois Nation, specifically the Seneca and Cayuga in the scorched earth march of 1779. They were joined by Brodhead, who ascended the Allegheny River from Pittsburgh into Seneca lands in northwestern Pennsylvania and southwestern New York.

1783

- Paris Peace Treaty, signed September 9. American and British delegations met in Paris, France, where Great Britain recognized the independence of the United States.

1784

- Cornplanter is a principle negotiator at Fort Stanwix (now Rome, New York) where the Iroquois Confederacy (Six Nations) and the United States made peace following the American Revolution. The Seneca ceded nearly a million acres of their homeland to the United States—without compensation—at this treaty *negotiation*. Also at this time, Pennsylvania purchased the remaining Iroquois lands in the Commonwealth.

1789

- Cornplanter is a principle negotiator at Fort Harmar (now Marietta, Ohio) where the Seneca supported the United States against the Indians of the Northwest Territory. The Iroquois present at these treaty negotiations agreed to sell the *Erie Triangle* for $2,000 worth of goods. At this time, Cornplanter thought that the fortunes and future of his people lay with the new government.

1790

- Cornplanter had extensive visits to Philadelphia to protest continued intrusion into Iroquois lands.

1791

- Land grants of Planters Field, including the two large river islands of Liberality and Donation, Richland, and the Gift to Seneca Chief Cornplanter and his heirs "for his valuable services to the whites."

1794

- Battle of Fallen Timbers—now diplomacy was the only tool left the Iroquois for peaceful negotiations with the whites and their ever-increasing westward expansion.
- Pickering Treaty of 1794. Colonel Pickering, George Washington's envoy to the Iroquois Confederacy, made this historic treaty with the Six Nations. At Canandaigua, the Six Nations gathered to ratify the treaty. This treaty played a pivotal role in the controversy surrounding the building of Kinzua Dam and the Allegheny Reservoir.

1798

- First Quakers arrived at the Cornplanter Grant on the upper Allegheny River. The estimated population at the Grant was four hundred Cornplanters living in thirty houses. These numbers are from *A Nineteenth-Century Journal of a Visit to the Indians of New York*, by Deardorff and Snyderman. Also included in this count were 3 horses, 14 horned cattle, 1 yoke of oxen, and 12 hogs. During this period the Allegheny River was used primarily for navigation, which included exploration, settlement, trade and commerce.

1801-1802

- Cornplanter visited Thomas Jefferson in Washington, D.C., to discuss Seneca land holdings.

1836

- February 18, Cornplanter died at home on his land grant on the Allegheny River, Warren County, Pennsylvania.

1848

- The Seneca Nation of Indians comes into formal existence following a political revolution which overthrew the corrupted chief system of government. The Seneca established a constitution, with elected officials in executive, legislative, and judiciary branches.

1871

- Legislative Act of March 23, Congress ends treaty making with the Indians.

1924

- Federal legislation makes all Indians U.S. citizens. The Citizenship Act of June, 1924, declared that all non-citizen Indians born within the territorial limits of the United States are citizens. The Citizenship Act was critical in the making of a 1959 Supreme Court decision regarding the taking of land from Indians. The Supreme Court concluded that Indian citizens could claim no special rights to retain their lands while the lands of other citizens were being condemned and taken as part of the Kinzua project.

1928

- First consideration of flood control on the Allegheny River by the U.S. Army Corps of Engineers.

1936

- Federal Flood Control Act. The federal role in flood control was expanded to include all navigable rivers of the nation.

1939

- U.S. Army Corps of Engineers did the first estimate of facts on construction of Kinzua Dam and the Allegheny Reservoir.

1940-1955

- Kinzua and upper Allegheny River flood control were not a priority due to World War II, and general public indifference to building the dam.

1956

- Record floods in March on the Allegheny and Ohio rivers greatly revived public interest in the building of Kinzua Dam.

1957

- January 11, the U.S. District Court for the Western District of New York upheld the government's right to condemn land of the Seneca Nation for the proposed Kinzua project.
- January 21, the U.S. Court of Appeals denied a petition of the Seneca Indians for a stay of the order of condemnation and possession of Seneca land previously granted to the federal government.
- U.S. Army Corps of Engineers agrees to have an independent engineering firm, TAMS, review the Seneca backed Morgan Plan, an alternate plan for flood control on the Allegheny and Ohio rivers. Subsequently, the Morgan Plan was rejected by the Army Corps of Engineers.

1958

- First federal appropriation of funds secured for Kinzua Dam construction.
- April 14, the U.S. District Court for the District of Columbia denied the Seneca Nation's request for an injunction to prevent the construction of Kinzua Dam and the Allegheny Reservoir.
- November 25, the U.S. Court of Appeals for the District of Columbia affirmed the April 14 action of the District Court in the injunction suit.

1959

- Opposition by Seneca Nation caused Congress to freeze appropriated monies pending court action. On June 15, the Supreme Court refused a motion by the Seneca Nation for a *writ of certiorari*. This Supreme Court action removed the last legal obstacle for construction of the dam.

1960

- Groundbreaking for Kinzua Dam occurred on October 22. State and federal officials broke ground in special ceremonies, which were attended by thousands of people. Ceremonies were at the western embankment site, home of the Brownell farm, which was soon to vanish.
- Village of Kinzua population: 1960, 458.
- Village of Corydon population: 1960, 165.
- 1960 census was the last official headcount in these vanished villages. Today, there are about 600 descendants of Cornplanter; the majority are enrolled members of the Seneca Nation of Indians.

1961

- Seneca Nation makes a last ditch appeal to President John F. Kennedy for another independent study to determine possible alternatives to the U.S. Army Corps of Engineers plan to flood one-third of their Allegany Reservation land. The Seneca letter of appeal was dated on George Washington's birthday, recalling promises from colonial times.

1962

- August 2, first concrete at the Kinzua Dam site was poured by the Hunkin-Conkey Company, Cleveland, Ohio.
- Route 59 bypass under construction by Latrobe Construction Company.
- Pennsylvania Railroad ends service along the Allegheny River road.
- Pennsylvania Electric Company (Penelec) seeks Kinzua Power Plant at site of Kinzua Dam.
- Slow death to village of Kinzua, as the government now owns much of the village.
- Jakes Rocks—recreational studies begin.
- National publicity increases on many fronts for support of Indian rights.

- Moving of graves begins in cemeteries to be flooded.
- Kinzua Post Office closed.
- Last services in Saint Luke's Episcopal Church, village of Kinzua.

1963

- February 18, the Allegheny River was diverted through the area that had been constructed within the first cofferdam.
- Last telephone call from Kinzua, residents take last look at Kinzua area.
- Corydon Post Office closes.
- Historical Society opens Indian mounds at Sugar Run.
- Kinzua Township to be merged with Mead Township.
- Fish hatchery creation at Kinzua Dam discussed.
- Clay seam in Kinzua Dam found.
- Corps of Engineers approves Penelec Kinzua Power Plant.
- President Johnson approves bill to continue Kinzua Dam work.

1964

- April, a long awaited Bureau of Outdoor Recreation report was released by the Secretary of the Interior, Stewart L. Udall. The report recommended that a national recreation area NOT be established around the reservoir because the area would stop at the New York State line and would not have a national character. The Allegany Reservation of the Seneca Nation surrounds the majority of the reservoir in New York State. It was also recommended that the federal lands to be developed around the reservoir for recreation be under the administration of the U.S. Forest Service.
- May 27, it was announced that the firm of Icanda, Ltd., Montreal, Canada, had been awarded a $2.3 million contract to build a cutoff wall that would correct the seepage condition found at the dam.
- Remaining Corydon families facing imminent eviction.
- Quaker Bridge, Onoville, and Red House Post Offices close.
- U.S. Forest Service receives the okay to manage the federal Kinzua Dam lands surrounding the reservoir.
- Kiasutha recreational area work begins.
- Bumper-to-bumper traffic visits dam site.

- Rim Rock recreational area dedicated.
- Relocated Route 59 officially opened November 25.
- Kinzua Valley clearing progresses in preparation for inundation by the water of the Allegheny Reservoir.
- Corydon Township to be consolidated into Mead Township, Warren County.

1965

- Work begins on the Penelec Kinzua Power Project. The Federal Power Commission granted a 50-year license to build and run a $40 million power plant at the dam to Cleveland Electric Illuminating Company (CEI) and Penelec.
- Fish Hatchery funds sought.
- Last concrete monolith closed at dam.

1966

- Construction began on the Seneca Power Plant in April.
- President Johnson's pen makes Kinzua Dam and Allegheny Reservoir name official now; bill was signed at the "Texas Whitehouse."
- Dedication of Kinzua Dam, September 16.

1969

- Seneca Power Plant was completed.

1972

- Summer: due to flood control by Kinzua Dam and the Allegheny Reservoir, the financial savings from the torrential rains associated with Hurricane Agnes were estimated at $247,000,000.

1973

- Severe corrosion of the dam's stilling basin concrete floor had been detected. Cause was determined to be the turbulent discharges of water from the dam.

1990

- The Allegheny Scenic Byway, a 31-mile stretch of Long House Drive, Route 59, and Route 321, was dedicated as part of the National Scenic Highway System.

- *No Kinzua Resort Coalition* based in Warren, Pennsylvania, vehemently opposed a plan to build a resort at Kinzua. The concept of a resort received little negative reaction before it was incorporated into the Forest Service Plans in 1987. Another round of similar conflict is certain as the Forest Service Plan is periodically revised.

- Twenty-five years after the completion of Kinzua Dam, the U.S. Corps of Engineers, which operates the dam, reports that the attraction was visited by 900,000 people between October, 1989, and October, 1990. Estimates were to be at least 1 million visitors, but consistently remain less.

2003

- As manufacturing employment declines, tourism and recreation are promoted on a local and regional basis.

- On New Year's Day a record-breaking northern pike was caught on the Allegheny Reservoir. A Bradford, Pennsylvania, man was ice fishing on the Allegheny Reservoir and landed the 35-pound fish, which measured 48 inches long and 21 ½ inches in girth. The Pennsylvania Fish and Boat Commission verified it as a state record.

- July, the annual Kinzua Classic Bike Race was held with nearly 180 cyclists from Pennsylvania, New York, Ohio, and other states participating.

- Throughout northwestern Pennsylvania the U.S. Forest Service held numerous public meetings regarding updates and revisions to the Allegheny National Forest Plan.

2004

- Northern Alleghenies Vacation Region (NAVR), Warren County's official tourism bureau and direct marketing organization, opens a new 3,600 square-foot visitors center west of the city of Warren.

Maps

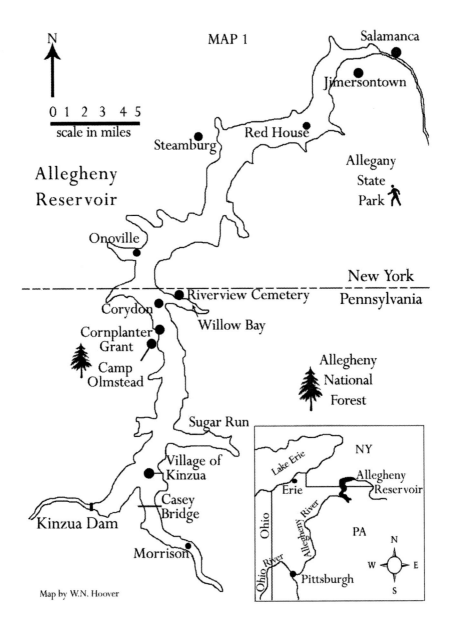

Map by W.N. Hoover

MAP 2

The Conewango-Cattaraugus Reservoir (Morgan Plan) shown with the authorized Kinzua Project. The Morgan Plan consisted of a low diversion dam on the Allegheny River to pass water in either direction, a dam on the Conewango Creek to create a reservoir, and an outlet-diversion channel and control works to let excess flood waters into Cattaraugus Creek and finally to flow into Lake Erie.

Map by W.N. Hoover

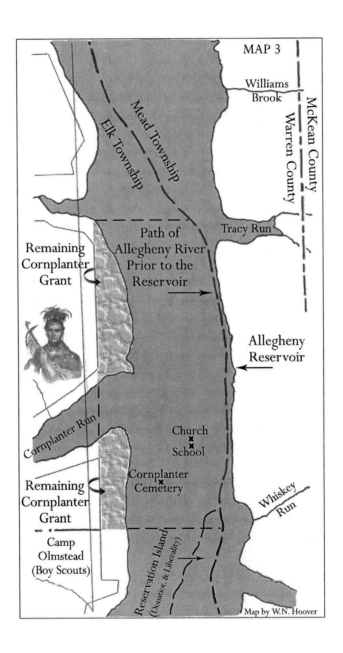

MAP 3

Williams Brook

McKean County
Warren County

Mead Township
Elk Township

Tracy Run

Path of
Allegheny River
Prior to the
Reservoir

Remaining
Cornplanter
Grant

Allegheny
Reservoir

Cornplanter Run

Church
School

Remaining
Cornplanter
Grant

Cornplanter
Cemetery

Whiskey Run

Camp
Olmstead
(Boy Scouts)

Reservation Island
(Donation & Liberality)

Map by W.N. Hoover

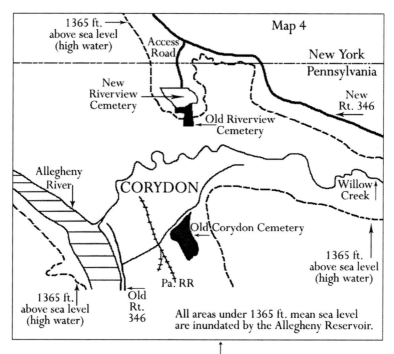

Map 4

1365 ft.
above sea level
(high water)

Access Road

New York
Pennsylvania

New Riverview Cemetery

New Rt. 346

Old Riverview Cemetery

Allegheny River

CORYDON

Willow Creek

Old Corydon Cemetery

1365 ft.
above sea level
(high water)

Pa. RR

1365 ft.
above sea level
(high water)

Old Rt. 346

All areas under 1365 ft. mean sea level
are inundated by the Allegheny Reservoir.

The old Corydon Cemetery and the old Riverview Cemetery were inundated by the Allegheny Reservoir. These cemeteries, plus the graves from the original Cornplanter Cemetery on the west bank of the Allegheny River, were moved to the new Riverview Cemetery. The old Corydon Cemetery had a recorded history from 1819 to 1963. It was originally established on land donated by Philip Tome, founder of Corydon, Pennsylvania.

Allegheny Reservoir

New York
Pennsylvania

Corydon

N
W ◆ E
S

Kinzua Dam

Map by W.N. Hoover

HISTORICAL PERSPECTIVE

A river's no mere artery of earth's, no aorta of the heartland, no petty sphygmic system spouting fishies for the hell of it: a river is *a trust:* exploitable: an invitation to a chance to channel, levee, riprap, tax and dam for profit. A river is a goldfield waiting to be panned. A purse. A cursive prayer to fortune. A course in economics.

–Evidence of Things Unseen, Marianne Wiggins

In most American hearts and minds, United States history formally dates from the year 1776, but the heritage of the land was already centuries old as the American colonies began their fight for independence. This founding heritage is Indian; complex, multi-dimensional cultures of explorers, warriors, poets, and statesmen. As certainly as the rich heritage of the continent and its indigenous people paved the way for the formation of the American colonies, the saga of Kinzua Dam in northwestern Pennsylvania began long before it was initially deliberated by the U.S. Army Corps of Engineers. *Kinzua—from Cornplanter to the Corps* is a story of power, intrigue, and conflict regarding one of the most controversial dams in the northeastern United States. Participants included great War Chiefs of the Iroquois Confederacy and Presidents of the United States, from George Washington to John F. Kennedy.

The historical record of the lands of the Iroquois Confederacy runs a long and remarkable course. While the focus of the construction of Kinzua Dam and the Allegheny Reservoir, with its associated political skirmishes and social upheaval, is on three decades of the 20th century—1936 to 1966—no perspective on this time period can be achieved without some understanding of the significant regional events of the early European-Americans and the Iroquois Indians of colonial America.

Prior to the arrival of the first European settlers the people who lived on the land that now comprises present-day Kinzua Dam and the Allegheny Reservoir were the Seneca Indians, the western most member nation of the Iroquois Confederacy—also the most numerous and powerful. The Seneca Indians once owned all of the lands in western New York and a portion of the state of Pennsylvania. The Seneca name for themselves is Tsonondowanenaka or Tsonondowaka meaning *People of the Great Hill or Mountain.* Over time the Seneca drifted into two groups, those in the Seneca Lake region and those on the Genesee River and upper Allegheny River. The western most Seneca were called the Chenussio people.

The original five Indian nations of the Iroquois Confederacy were the Seneca, Cayuga, Onondaga, Oneida, and Mohawk. During the 1720s the Tuscarora refugees from North Carolina were admitted to the Confederacy as an associate member under the sponsorship of the Oneida; for this reason the Iroquois Confederacy—the League of Five Nations—is also known as the League of Six Nations. The Iroquois also call themselves the Haudenosaunee, the *People of the Longhouse.*

With incidental exceptions, the history of the Seneca, prior to the American Revolution, is virtually that of the Iroquois Confederacy. This confederacy of powerful Indian nations was created to bring peace, and all nations operated under an unwritten code of conduct known as the Great Law of Peace.

The nations of the Iroquois Confederacy possessed vast lands that were immensely rich in resources, both natural and cultural. These resources had a varied and beneficial impact on the European-Americans arriving in the Great Lakes region. The territory of the Seneca Nation, the keepers of the western door of the Iroquois Confederacy, possessed a system of lakes and rivers that created a natural gateway to the interior of the continent; consequently, these Seneca lands were key to westward expansion for European explorers and settlers.

In the early days of the Revolutionary War both the British and the Americans formally urged the Iroquois to maintain neutrality, while each covertly acted to have the Six Nations aligned with them. At the continued urging of the British, the Iroquois Confederacy, with a majority rule among their own leaders, went to war against the American colonies. The Iroquois entered the Revolutionary War and militarily aligned themselves with the British; a fateful decision made July of 1777 at Oswego—a trading post on the south shore of Lake Ontario. The Oneida and the Tuscarora declined to take up the hatchet against the rebel American colonies. This decision split the Iroquois Confederacy for the Oneida and Tuscarora were now defined as dissenting nations. The continuance of a policy of military neutrality was impossible—the die was cast irrevocably.

In post-Revolutionary War times the Iroquois were virtually abandoned by the defeated British. The British, no longer willing or able to follow up on their wartime promises to the Iroquois, left them to deal on their own with the victorious colonies. This was not an easy task for the Iroquois Confederacy due to the great push westward by pioneers. At the close of the American War of Independence, pioneers were most eager to settle along water-ways of the western frontier, and to obtain the rich and wild lands of the Iroquois Nation. Lands west of the Allegheny Mountains were the new frontier—land of the Iroquois Confederacy.

Emerging from the turbulent times of the Revolutionary War was a dynamic leader of the Seneca Nation, Cornplanter. Having fought with the British and lost, and now abandoned by them, Cornplanter soon realized that cooperating with the new nation was the best way to help his people, and to preserve the remnants of their lands. Through these efforts Cornplanter became a powerful and respected leader of his people. His struggles and victories echoed through the centuries, and played a pivotal part in the Kinzua Dam controversy more that a century and a half later. *How this came to be warrants a closer look.*

Cornplanter, born about 1750, was half Indian. He was born to a Seneca Indian mother of some prominence. She was a member of the Wolf Clan. An individual's clan identification is an essential element of Seneca social and cultural life.

All Seneca Indians are members of one of eight clans: the Wolf, the Turtle, the Bear, the Beaver, the Deer, the Heron, the Snipe, and the Hawk. The clans are traditionally divided into two groups of four clans. These groups are called moieties. One moiety consists of the Wolf, the Turtle, the Bear, and the Beaver. The other moiety consists of the Deer, the Heron, the Snipe, and the Hawk. Believers of the Handsome Lake or Longhouse religion rely on these traditional organizations. The moieties still operate today in a religious context when certain ceremonies and clan duties need to be performed.

The clans of the Seneca were of primary importance as the social, political, and religious life of each member—each family—was built upon this common foundation. Ideally in Seneca life, members of the same clan may not marry. Among the Seneca an individual inherits his clan through the mother—this matrilineal system continues today. Cornplanter followed this tradition and was a member of the Wolf Clan, as was his Seneca mother. Cornplanter thought of himself this way—with his birthrights traced through his mother—and he lived fully as a Seneca Indian.

Cornplanter's father was an American of Dutch descent named John Abeel (A'beel), whose father had once been mayor of Albany, New York. John Abeel, not at all satisfied with established life in Albany, left to explore the wilderness, where he met and wed Cornplanter's mother. He was a trader among the Indians for a number of years. It was John Abeel's unique skill as a gunsmith that allowed his passage among the Indians. The British and the French had provided arms to the Indians, but anyone who could repair them was always welcomed.

On the colonial frontier, the Dutch name, Abeel, was altered by mispronunciation to O'Bail. Cornplanter took this as the American form of his name for the rest of his life. In his youth, he was also called the Seneca equivalent of Johnny. Later in life, because of his strong avocation of improved farming methods for the Senecas, he was named Gy-ant-wa-chia, meaning *One Who Plants* or *By What One Plants*. This in turn was twisted by his English friends into Cornplanter. Here he will be referred to as Cornplanter, as this is the name best known to history.

As a young warrior Cornplanter was powerful, aggressive, and often victorious in combat. As a young man, he reportedly had killed several men in numerous battles. It is critical to understand that Cornplanter was not by descent a chief of the Seneca. He became a *Head Warrior* as the result of his ability and strength of character. Cornplanter *achieved* this status as a leader—it was not merely ascribed to him by birth right. Cornplanter established his right to represent his people, even in treaty negotiations where all Six Nations were represented. In many ways Cornplanter was a self-made man. He proved over many decades to be farsighted and skilled in his dealings with the whites.

A true tale, often recorded, is that in one Revolutionary War raid Cornplanter captured his father, John Abeel. The father did not recognize his son, and he was without a doubt much surprised when, after being marched for several miles, Cornplanter introduced himself. This encounter is much noted in historical journals and the consensus is that Cornplanter's introduction went as follows:

> My name is John Abeel, commonly called Cornplanter. I am your son. You are now my prisoner, and subject to the custom of Indian warfare; but you shall not be harmed.
>
> You need not fear. I am a warrior. Many are the scalps I have taken. Many prisoners have I tortured to death.
>
> I was anxious to see you and greet you in friendship. I went to your cabin and took you by force; but your life shall be spared.
>
> If you now choose to follow the fortunes of your yellow son I will cherish your old age with plenty of venison, and you shall live easy. But if it is your choice to return to your fields and live with your white children, I will send a party of trusty young men to conduct you back safely.

John Abeel decided not to stay with his Indian son in the forest. He was safely returned to his home by the Seneca.

After the Revolutionary War, Cornplanter requested help for his people from George Washington and from the Quaker Society of Philadelphia. This would not have been painless to do, as Cornplanter was a War Chief who had fought on the side of the British in the Revolutionary War and lost. In the post-war time period, in an effort to aid his people, Cornplanter demonstrated many peaceful qualities of leadership that won him the respect and admiration of George Washington. One of Cornplanter's crucial goals at this time was the preservation of the remaining lands of the Seneca after their defeat in the Revolutionary War.

In this post-war time, both the newly emerging American government and the Quaker Society were centered in Philadelphia, Pennsylvania. Cornplanter visited Philadelphia many times on trips representing the wellbeing and interests of his people. With the new American government he strived to protect the remaining Seneca lands; and of the Quakers, he requested help in educating his people. In 1798, the Quakers accepted Cornplanter's appeal; help was provided in education, farming, and construction. Cornplanter knew that to survive on the land that remained to them, the Seneca would need to learn new skills and ways of life.

The Quakers worked diligently to protect the best interests of the Cornplanter Indians and played an integral part in their negotiations with the American

Government in post-Revolutionary times. Being true and supportive of the Cornplanters became a point of honor with the Philadelphia Quakers.

In 1791, in gratitude for Indian assistance and diplomacy in the years following the end of the American Revolution, Cornplanter was given three tracts of land by the Pennsylvania General Assembly. One of these tracts was a grant of land on the upper Allegheny River in Warren County—land that would eventually be taken back more than a century and a half later, by that very same government, for construction of a large and controversial dam. It is essential to understand that these lands were given to Cornplanter in perpetuity. These lands were not an Indian reservation. This is a critical distinction. The grant was the property of Cornplanter and his heirs alone.

Cornplanter's most important service to the white settlers at this time was his actions in preventing the Iroquois Nations from joining the Confederacy of Western Indians in 1790-1791, the war which terminated in the victory of General Wayne at Fallen Timbers in 1794. General Wayne's victory opened up lands west of the Allegheny Mountains to pioneer settlers.

If the Iroquois had joined the efforts in resisting westward expansion it is most probable that General Wayne would not have been victorious at Fallen Timbers and lands west of the Iroquois, such as Ohio, would not have been opened to settlers. Undoubtedly Cornplanter's efforts to protect his people were frequently done at great personal cost and anguish. Strong leaders were needed, and these were difficult and dangerous times.

Thanks to the Pennsylvania General Assembly, Cornplanter had his tracts of land, but the land holdings of the Iroquois Confederacy were not yet determined by the colonial government in 1791. The Iroquois Confederacy negotiated the Canandaigua Treaty of 1794 with the United States of America to determine its land holdings. The treaty was signed by President George Washington on November 11, 1794. Congress approved the Treaty of 1794 in Philadelphia on January 21, 1795.

Representing George Washington in these treaty negotiations was his commissioner to the Indians, Colonel Timothy Pickering. Accompanying Colonel Pickering was General Israel Chapin. Often the treaty is referred to as the Pickering Treaty, the Canandaigua Treaty of 1794 (the year it was negotiated and signed by George Washington), and the Treaty of 1795 (the year Congress approved it). For the purposes of *Kinzua* it is referred to as the Treaty of 1794 in honor of those who negotiated and signed it in good faith.

Also present at the treaty negotiations was William Savery, a Quaker from Philadelphia, Pennsylvania. William Savery attended the Treaty Council to assist the Six Nations in their negotiations with the United States. Friends (Quakers) served as interpreters on behalf of the Indians. The primary negotiators included the following from the Iroquois Confederacy: Farmer Brother, Red Jacket, Little Billy, and Cornplanter from the Seneca Nation; Fish Carrier from the Cayuga Nation; and Clear Sky from the Onondaga Nation.

The Treaty of 1794 grants the Seneca Indians exclusive rights to their reservation lands. During the Kinzua controversy this treaty served as the basis of the Seneca Nation of Indians' argument that the federal government had no right to usurp the Indian lands for construction of the Kinzua Dam.

The Treaty of 1794 states in part:

> Now, the United States acknowledges all the land within the aforementioned boundaries, to be the property of the Seneka nation; and the United States will never claim the same, nor disturb the Seneka nation, nor any of the Six Nations, or any of their Indian friends residing thereon and united with them, in the free use and enjoyment thereof; but it shall remain theirs, until they choose to sell the same to the people of the United States, who have the right to purchase.
>
> *~From Article III, Treaty of November 11, 1794.*

("Seneka" spelling true to the treaty.)

The treaty was signed by 59 Sachems and War Chiefs of the Six Nations. Timothy Pickering, representing President George Washington, signed for the United States. Today, this is the oldest treaty to which the United States is a party and which is still in force.

In 1960, most people living in Pennsylvania or even in Warren County, Pennsylvania—home of Cornplanter—were unaware that a band of Indians still lived on ancestral land near the headwaters of the Allegheny River, and had been there since 1791! This was the cherished land given to Cornplanter for his valued services to the newly formed United States of America.

In the mid-twentieth century, this small group of fifty families gave insomnia to federal and state legislators and to an army of engineers eager to start construction on the proposed Kinzua Dam and Allegheny Reservoir. The property of these Indian families, the soil on which they had lived and buried their families for hundreds of years, lie in the way of the engineers' project. Since this land was given in perpetuity to the descendants of Cornplanter, it did not belong to the

United States government, or to the state of Pennsylvania. The Seneca insisted that the land could not be condemned or confiscated against their wishes.

Construction of the Kinzua Dam and the Allegheny Reservoir required the taking of both the Cornplanter Grant land—the last Indian land in Pennsylvania—and Seneca Nation Reservation land in New York State. No Seneca desired to sell their land. The land was taken; even though the Treaty of 1794 states that the United States would never claim the land unless the Seneca chose to sell to the people of the United States.

On April 14, 1958, the U.S. District Court for the District of Columbia ruled that the U.S. Army Corps of Engineers could take reservation land by the right of eminent domain. The implication clearly was that if the United States government could make a treaty, it could also break a treaty. The oldest Indian treaty in existence was dishonored and became the object of much concern, controversy, and debate. The case went to the U.S. Court of Appeals for the District of Columbia and to the U.S. Supreme Court, but the judgment against the Indians stood.

In 1963, during the hearings before the Subcommittee of Indian Affairs, House of Representatives, Eighty-Eighth Congress, Representative Haley (Florida) expressed his concern about the vital responsibility that the U.S. Army Corps of Engineers in particular, and the U.S. Government in general, have to the Seneca Nation. The following statement by Mr. Haley was addressed to numerous members of the U.S. Corps of Engineers, including Woodrow L. Berge, Acting Director of Real Estate, Office of Chief of Engineers, and Colonel Bert De Melker, District Engineer, U.S. Army Engineer District, Pittsburgh, Pennsylvania.

Representative Haley said:

> The Seneca Nation took the Army Corps of Engineers to the Supreme Court, and the Supreme Court, without directly ruling on the situation of whether the Congress of the United States intended to take Indian lands, in a weaseling opinion that they rendered, not going directly to the question, merely said that the appropriation by Congress of money for the start of construction was evidence that the Congress intended to take the Indian lands.

> I might say to the gentlemen also that this project violates and absolutely throws out the window a treaty signed in 1794 with this tribe of Indians, ratified by the Senate of the United States, and signed by the first President of this great Republic, George

Washington, who in turn felt so keenly about the treaty that later on he wrote a letter to the great Indian chief, Cornplanter, saying that this land would never be taken by the U.S. Government except by the Seneca Nation's willingness to sell, which of course they have never been willing to do.

Briefly, it violates the oldest active treaty that the United Sates has in existence today. It violates a treaty that the Senate of the United States ratified. At a time when we are talking about people who will not keep their commitments, I think this is one of the most flagrant violations that has ever come to my attention.

With that background, I think the gentleman will understand how I feel about this particular project. Our Nation has received tremendous criticism about this dam. If we allow this matter to drag on, and if we close those gates and these Indians do not have some place to go, if the Army Corps of Engineers has not relocated these Indians, we will be subject to a tremendous amount of criticism all over the United States, and justly so.

That is the reason I have urged and I continue to urge that the Army Corps of Engineers proceed as rapidly as they possibly can to relocate these people and to build the necessary roads. As the gentlemen can see, when they have completed this project, they have taken the heart completely out of the Seneca Nation Reservation. They might as well have taken the rest of the land, because it leaves them mountainsides, and that is about all.

Once the bureaucratic wheels of the U.S. Corps of Engineers were set into motion, they were impossible to reverse. Along with the taking of Cornplanter Grant land and Seneca Reservation land, the property of many non-Indians was also taken by eminent domain. Entire towns were cleared and their denizens relocated. The inundating of these valleys and their long-established towns and villages with water is also the story of *Kinzua*, for today these towns live only in memory. Gone are Kinzua, Corydon, Red House, Quaker Bridge, Morrison, Onoville, one-third of the Allegany Reservation, the Cornplanter Grant—only a strong feeling of nostalgia remains as these names are recalled. Also required was the federal acquisition of miles of railroad, highways, and power lines.

In these valleys of the upper Allegheny River something ancient and natural is undeniably gone forever. In its place are Kinzua Dam and the Allegheny Reservoir.

To include the devastating destruction of the homes, towns, and ways of life valued for centuries, without including the many facets of the actual construction of the dam would be remiss and would tell only part of the story.

History also records that America is a land of builders, and in its building it is large, forceful, and ever ambitious. This is predominantly true for the practices of the U.S. Army Corps of Engineers, the builders of Kinzua Dam. How does a huge, costly, and controversial project such as this come into existence? A project such as Kinzua Dam could not come into being solely on the recommendations of the Corps of Engineers. A project such as this is initiated by the people in the affected areas. Who were these people and how did such a massive undertaking begin?

The U.S. Army Corps of Engineers, by Congressional directive, investigates and reports. The Corps decided the dam was the best means for achieving the desired objective—flood protection and associated water resource development for the Upper Ohio River Basin—and concluded that the proposed Allegheny Reservoir provided the best and most economical means for controlling and utilizing the water resources of the upper Allegheny River. Favorable reports from the Corps, in the case of Kinzua Dam, resulted in approval by Congress. The Kinzua Dam and Allegheny Reservoir project was formally authorized by the Flood Control Acts of June 22, 1936; June 28, 1938; and August 18, 1941. This was the meeting of high water and politics.

To say that emotions soared during the heated debate on whether or not to pursue the dam would be an understatement. The disparate opinions on the building of the dam are exemplified in the following two quotes. The first is by Seneca Nation of Indians leader, George D. Heron, as testified at a House Interior subcommittee hearing on a proposal to force Army engineers to consider alternatives to the Kinzua Dam project, said to endanger the Allegany Reservation.

> This project (Kinzua Dam) will flood the heart of our reservation homeland, which we Senecas have peacefully occupied since the treaty of November 11, 1794. I know it will sound simple and perhaps silly, but the truth of the matter is that my people really believe that George Washington read the 1794 treaty before he signed, and that he meant exactly what he wrote.... To us it is more than a contract, more than a symbol to us; the 1794 treaty is a way of life.

On the opposite end of the spectrum was Pennsylvania Governor David L. Lawrence speaking the week before groundbreaking for the dam.

> Few projects in Western Pennsylvania will ever benefit millions
> in so many ways as this new dam at Kinzua—a project for which
> so many of us have been fighting for over the years.

Many communities from Warren to Pittsburgh enthusiastically supported and lobbied for the dam, while there were many groups that supported the Indian effort and the struggles of those who resided in the small towns and villages, such as Kinzua and Corydon, which were soon to vanish.

On April 29, 1957, the *Pittsburgh Sun-Telegraph* quoted two engineers as saying the proposed dam at Kinzua may not be the most feasible or economical flood control program for the Allegheny River. The newspaper quoted Dr. Arthur E. Morgan, former head of the Tennessee Valley Authority, and his associate, Barton Jones:

> It seems clear to us that the permanent and complete removal of
> flood waters from the upper Allegheny can be accomplished by
> diversion, with greater benefits of every kind than would be
> accomplished by the construction of the Kinzua Dam, and
> probably at very substantially less cost.

These alternatives to the proposed Kinzua Dam were known as the Morgan Plan, of which there were several variations. Morgan proposed diverting the flood waters of the Allegheny River into Lake Erie by using a series of smaller dams. *(See Map 2.)*

Colonel H. E. Sprague, Chief of the U.S. Army Corps of Engineers in Pittsburgh, said that the proposal to divert Allegheny River flood waters into Lake Erie was not economical. On May 15, 1957, Congressman L. H. Gavin, 23rd District, Pennsylvania, in a statement before the Public Works Subcommittee of the House Appropriations Committee, regarding the Allegheny River Reservoir project, said:

> As the Committee is aware, an alternative diversion plan has
> been proposed…and under no circumstances would we be
> interested in any diversion proposals to divert the excess water
> into Lake Erie as this water is needed for the domestic and
> industrial life of the Allegheny Valley, and the City of Pittsburgh

with its 1 and ½ million people. Our objective is to harness and retain the water for use in the Allegheny Valley and not divert it to Lake Erie.

On October 22, 1960, ground was formally broken for the $119 million Kinzua Dam with a completion date set for 1966. The philosophical purpose inherent to the designers of the dam was best explained by John F. Kennedy:

> The American, by nature, is optimistic. He is experimental, an inventor and a builder who builds best when called upon to build greatly.

Today the Kinzua Dam and the Allegheny Reservoir constitute the most important unit in the Allegheny-Ohio River system for the protection of every town from the tail waters of the dam to the city of Pittsburgh, and onward to the upper Ohio River Valley. In many ways the saga of the upper Allegheny River, Chief Cornplanter, and the Kinzua Valley is the chronicle, to a great extent, of America. This is most assuredly true today as populations continue to shift, and new economies struggle to be invented, altering the paths communities have followed in their distant and recent histories. Today there is a fight for rebirth in many communities of the upper Allegheny River—a great effort to redefine themselves in difficult economic times—hopefully, with a sense of optimism and a sound historical perspective for guidance.

THE WHIPPOORWILL CRIES

Throughout our history few Americans have understood the American Indian concept of land. It seems eminently fair to most Americans to take land as long as it is paid for. To the Senecas and to most American Indians land is not compensable. The land is your mother. You do not sell you mother.

~ Testimony during the hearings before the Subcommittee on Indian Affairs, House of Representatives, 88th Congress, 1963.

The reservation is not merely a repository of a dwindling heritage. It is, also, a society in which new possibilities of Indian cultural expression struggle to establish themselves. To the Indian, the land of the reservation is a material segment of an ancient tradition, and the basis and focus for his identity as an Indian.

~Memorandum to House Resolution 1794 from the hearings before the Subcommittee on Indian Affairs, 1963.

A traditional Seneca saying is that when the whippoorwill cries in the east, close by the house, some evil will befall the family; when a fox is heard whimpering in the woods, a death will follow.

In 1790, Cornplanter visited Philadelphia to protest inroads by pioneers into Iroquois lands. Upon this visit, despite his protests, Cornplanter was assured by George Washington that protection for his people was forthcoming. At this time, Cornplanter characterized George Washington as a *town destroyer*, recalling Washington's 1779 military campaign against his people, which destroyed crops, orchards, and decimated Indian settlements.

This significant military campaign into Iroquois country under General Washington was a three-prong attack which consumed a great deal of Washington's military efforts for 1779. First, General James Clinton, with 1,600 men, descended the Susquehanna River from Otsego Lake in New York State, destroying several Tuscarora settlements along the way. Clinton then joined forces with General John Sullivan—the second prong of the attack. Sullivan ascended the Susquehanna River to meet Clinton at Tioga, present-day Athens, Pennsylvania. The combined forces of Clinton and Sullivan totaled 5,000 men. Under Sullivan's command, the troops proceeded with a scorched earth military campaign—west into Cayuga and Seneca lands. Forty Indian towns were destroyed in the combined Clinton-Sullivan march, and as many as 160,000 bushels of corn were lost by the Cayuga and Seneca. At nearly the same time General David Brodhead was forming the third prong of the attack. Brodhead ascended the Allegheny River from Pittsburgh into the Seneca land in northwestern Pennsylvania and southwestern New York. With as many as 600 men he proceeded to destroy Indian towns and settlements. Much that was good and productive was laid to waste by Washington's 1779 campaign, and recovery for the Iroquois required years. Many Iroquois women and children spent much of 1780 under the protection of the British at Niagara, while Iroquois fighters continued an effective guerilla-type offensive in their homelands. This type of warfare worked very well for the Iroquois. Without a doubt, the cries of the whippoorwill were heard across the Seneca Nation.

In a 1790 address to President Washington, Cornplanter explained why the Seneca fought with England, and against the Americans. He explained that in the beginning the colonists told the Indians that they were the children of one great Father—the king of England. This Father had invited the Seneca to accept his protection and to obey him as the Indians were all regarded as his children. In his address to President Washington, Cornplanter continued his explanation:

What the Seneca Nation promise, they faithfully perform. When you refused to obey that King, he commanded us to assist his beloved men in making you sober. In obeying him, we did no more than yourselves had led us to promise. We were deceived; but your people teaching us to confide in that King, had helped to deceive us, and we now appeal to your heart. Is all the blame ours?

Cornplanter was not always a friend of the colonial Americans—though he assisted greatly in settling complicated Indian relations with the newly formed Republic after the Revolutionary War. In fact, there was little the Iroquois could do to stop the westward encroachment of white settlers, but Cornplanter did find himself in the position to influence the destiny of much of the western frontier, which at this time were lands west of the Allegheny Mountains. This westward expansion was a major concern in the critical years following the American Revolution. Essentially the government was broke and in debt due to the costs of the war, but the government did have land. This newly formed government and the lives of thousands of pioneers hinged on the critical settlement of these western lands, and Cornplanter proved to be an outstanding statesman for his people. His policies were often pursued at great personal cost. These decisions were seen by Cornplanter as the only way to prevent the total extinction of his people. Later Cornplanter grew to doubt the benefit of these policies in dealing with the settlers and the government.

Cornplanter, in his later years, made his home at Junishadago (Burnt House), also known as Cornplanter Town. It was located on the mainland tract of the Cornplanter Grant known as Planters Field. Descriptions of this village as it appeared at the time of Cornplanter can be had from the writings of numerous historians. It is generally described as being in one of the more rugged sections of the Allegheny River. It was usually reached by canoe. Some sixty-odd acres had been cleared on the river-bottom land, and some four hundred persons, living in thirty houses, made up its population at its peak. This was the most important of the Seneca towns on the upper Allegheny. At one time or another, it was home to nearly every Seneca leader. Junishadago was the objective in 1779 of Colonel Brodhead's punitive expedition, which burned several Indian villages, their crops, and killed many Seneca warriors.

Cornplanter's house, which served as a guest house, a ceremonial center, and a home for his family, was really two houses set about ten feet apart. Each house was sixteen feet wide and about thirty feet long. They were built of poles and covered in bark. An outstanding example of this type of construction can be viewed at the Seneca-Iroquois National Museum in Salamanca, New York.

When Reverend Timothy Alden, head of Allegheny College, visited Cornplanter in 1816, he found the village in flourishing condition. He reported:

> Cornplanter's village is on a handsome piece of bottom land, and comprises about a dozen buildings. I was grateful to acknowledge the agricultural habits of the place, and the numerous enclosures of buckwheat, corn and oats.
>
> We saw a number of oxen, cows and horses, and many logs designed for the sawmill and the Pittsburgh market. Last year the Western Missionary Society established a school in the village.

Reverend Alden described Cornplanter as about 68 years of age at this time. His face was strongly marked with intelligence. His house was "of princely dimensions, compared with most Indian huts, and has a piazza in front." According to Dr. Alden the name Kinzua means "Place of Many Fishes."

Cornplanter had six children, one of whom predeceased him. Charles O'Bail was the last son of Cornplanter. He claimed to have been born during the *Big War*, meaning the Revolutionary War.

Handsome Lake (Skaniadariyo or sometimes Ganiodayo) was a half-brother of Cornplanter. It was on the Cornplanter Grant that Handsome Lake had his visions of the Four Prophets which led to the establishment of what is known today as the Code of Handsome Lake. These beliefs are still followed by some Iroquois today in the Long Houses of the Great Lakes region and in Canada.

Having been a notable user of alcohol, Handsome Lake, after his visions and consequent sobriety, was a great promoter of temperance. His Code represents an extremely high ethical standard of belief, behavior, and thanksgiving. There is little doubt that the *Good Message*, the Gaiwiio, of Handsome Lake was responsible for the survival of the Seneca Indians in the early 19th century during a period of enormous difficulty.

HANDSOME LAKE

Home of Handsome Lake, the Seneca prophet, was across the river. There in 1799 the Four Messengers gave the Creator's blessing and sanction to found the new Indian religion bearing his name.

Allegheny River view of the Cornplanter Grant, 1940.

Cornplanter also lectured strongly for temperance. Merle Deardorff, Warren County historian, noted that Warren's Judge S. P. Johnson, in a letter to the *Oil City Derrick* in 1878 said:

> He (Cornplanter) was the original temperance man of western Pennsylvania, the life-long and persistent enemy of the white man's fire water, and not only abstained himself, but did everything in his power to discourage its use.

A speech by Cornplanter, a classic example of Indian eloquence, said in part:

> The Great Spirit first made the world and next the flying animals, and found all things good and prosperous. After finishing the flying animals He came down to earth and there stood. Then He made different kinds of trees, and weeds of all sort; and people of every kind. He made the Spring and other seasons and the weather suitable for planting. These He did make.
>
> But stills, to make whiskey to be given to Indians, He did not make.
>
> When the Great Sprit had made the earth and its animals He went into the great lakes, where He breathes as easily as anywhere else and then made all the different kinds of fish. The different kinds of things He made to be separate. The different animals He made not to mix with or disturb each other. But the white people have broken His command by mixing their colors with the Indians. The Indians have done better by not doing so.

Deardorff noted that Cornplanter and his half-brother, Handsome Lake, were certainly the most famous orators ever heard in Warren County.

In 1795, the Quaker Committee, Indian Committee of the Philadelphia Yearly Meeting of Friends, was founded. Its mission was to aid the Iroquois Confederacy by offering their services to Cornplanter and his people.

On January 5, 1796, the Quaker Committee sent a message to the Six Nations expressing its thankfulness that the Indians were at peace, and advising that they had received messages from the chiefs stating the Indians could no longer live by hunting. The Quaker Committee asked whether the Indians wished to be taught farming and other useful trades, and whether they wanted their children to learn to read and write. The Committee reiterated the fact that the Quakers had no designs on Indian lands.

Timothy Pickering, Secretary of State at this time, agreed with the Quakers' view on farming and education, and on February 15, 1796, recommended the Quaker Plan as "better calculated to procure lasting and essential benefits to your nations than any plan ever before attempted...." Pickering also stated that the Quakers would seek "no payment in furs, land, or money" for the services rendered, according to the papers of *A Nineteenth-Century Journal of a Visit to the Indians of New York*, proceedings of the American Philosophical Society, 1956, Mearle H. Deardorff and George S. Snyderman.

Cornplanter maintained his contact with the Quakers of Philadelphia, and his desire for help for his people remained a constant. In addition to agriculture, Cornplanter stressed the education of his people as a priority. This was perhaps his most important post-war contribution to his people.

On November 23, 1798, the first school opened in Cornplanter's home and the Quaker Henry Simmons ran the school. The going was tough. According to early records, when the weather was bad the school was full, and when the weather was good it was often empty. Soon the school moved from Cornplanter's home, as a small schoolhouse, attended by both children and adults, was built this same year, 1798. During the early 19th century the school did not operate every year as there were periods of turmoil and unrest which forced short-term closings of the school.

In *A Nineteenth-Century Journal of a Visit to the Indians of New York*, Deardorff and Snyderman noted that often in the evenings Henry Simmons sat with the Indian men and tried to answer many of the questions the Indians had about the whites and their ways. Especially thorny for Simmons to explain was how the whites reconciled their religious professions with their treatment of the Indians. Such problematic questions as: "Was it right for whites and Indians to marry since each went to a different Heaven (or Hell) when he died? What happened to the half-breed children? Why, if the Bible was intended for Indians, hadn't it been fixed so the Indians could read it?" Explaining such contradictions and shortfalls in the ways of the white man would not have been an enviable task for anyone.

In 1802, Cornplanter visited Thomas Jefferson at Monticello. Cornplanter had gained the attention of Jefferson for his emphasis on agriculture, education, and temperance. Jefferson urged him to continue this work. It had now become Cornplanter's mission among his people.

Cornplanter's allegiance to the United States at this point in time was still very strong and was to remain so for more than a decade. It may be best exemplified by his march with 200 warriors to Franklin, Pennsylvania, in 1812. Cornplanter and his warriors wished to join in the battle against Great Britain—once his ally against the United States. His services were declined by the U.S. Government. Cornplanter's son, Henry, did fight in the War of 1812, and received the rank of Major.

Around 1818, Cornplanter started to become disillusioned with the whites and their government, as many of his dealings with them were marked by trickery and outright deceit. Slowly, but inevitably, he became more disheartened: for example, when Cornplanter sold his 500-acre grant in Oil City, it was said he was paid with worthless bank papers. Though he tried for many years, Cornplanter was unable to obtain any satisfaction from the parties involved in this land dealing.

In 1822 Warren County attempted to collect taxes on the Cornplanter Grant on the upper Allegheny River. Cornplanter resisted paying the taxes, threatened force, but eventually paid the demanded tax dollars of $43.79. He appealed to the governor of Pennsylvania and the funds were returned with the promise of no further taxation by the county of Warren.

Cornplanter's discontent with dealing with the white man grew, and he continued to withdraw from their way of life. The school on the Grant was closed for some time. He destroyed the medals and the uniform that George Washington had presented to him at an earlier time. This divide widened as Cornplanter continued to further separate himself in his later years from the customs of the white man's way of life.

In 1857, a $200 grant was given by the Pennsylvania State Legislature for the construction of a new school building on the Cornplanter Grant. The small 1798 schoolhouse built by the Cornplanters was no longer useful. Marsh Pierce, a noteworthy Cornplanter, built the new state-supplied, wooden school. This school opened in September of 1857. In this same year the state legislature also introduced a bill appropriating $100 yearly for the operation of the school. Miss Juliet Leadeth Tome, eighteen years of age, was the first teacher at this new school. She was paid sixteen dollars monthly for her work. She boarded with the Marsh Pierce family on the Grant. Boarding with a family was common practice, as the weather made travel impossible much of the time. To her credit Miss Tome learned much of the Seneca language during her stay.

Above, Miss Juliet Leadeth Tome, first teacher at the 1857 Cornplanter School. Below, Miss Lucia Browne, the last teacher at the 1903 brick school, with some of her class.

By 1903, the 1857 wooden schoolhouse needed to be replaced. At this time, the Pennsylvania State Legislature appropriated up to $3000 for a new brick schoolhouse. Bricks for the school were shipped by railroad to the town of Corydon, which was located east of the school and across the Allegheny River. Bricks were transported on sleds across the river in winter, when the ice was thick enough. The school, built by George Lott of Warren, was finished in 1903. The first state-supplied public schoolhouse, built of wood by Marsh Pierce in 1857, was occupied as a cabin as late as 1941 by Marsh's youngest son, Windsor.

Miss Lucia Browne taught at the 1903 brick school the longest. She was there for the 1912-13 school year. She returned in 1930 and remained through 1953. The school provided a second floor apartment for its state-supplied teacher. Her grandmother, Miss Juliet Leadeth Tome, was the first state teacher and Miss Lucia Browne was the last. These facts about the school were gathered from Lucia Browne's personal copy of the pamphlet, *Cornplanter Grant in Warren County*, by Mearle Deardorff.

Douglas & Harry Jacobs at the Cornplanter School, above.
School is abandoned, ready for bulldozers, below.

By the year 1940 annual grants for the school had been gradually increased from $300 to $1500. Facts gathered from the *Warren County Review, 1739-1950,* by H.L. Blair, Warren County Superintendent during the 1950s, show that the Warren County School District census records report the attendance at the school was 81 in 1900; 77 in 1910; 35 in 1920; 34 in 1930; and 36 in 1940. The Cornplanter School was closed December 31, 1953. A decade later, the building of Kinzua Dam required the demolition of Pennsylvania's last Indian school.

Quakers had long been associated with the Cornplanter Grant, but by 1815 they were joined by the Western Missionary Society. The Society had worked to establish a presence on the Cornplanter Grant, and had sent a missionary named Samuel Oldham. The Society was sporadically active at Jennesadaga, Cornplanter Town, until April 10, 1883. At that time a new Allegheny and Cornplanter Presbyterian Church was enrolled by the Buffalo Presbytery. It was dedicated on September 17, 1885.

The church was built on land set aside for community use when the Grant was partitioned among the heirs of Cornplanter in 1871. At dedication time, September 17, 1885, ninety people from Warren took the 9:15 a.m. flyer up the railroad tracks along the Allegheny River, and unloaded at Johnny Cake railroad station on the eastern bank of the Allegheny River, opposite the Cornplanter Grant. Cornplanter Indians ferried the guests across the river in johnboats. The visitors returned to Warren on the 6:30 p.m. train.

The Reverend Perry S. Allen delivered the dedication speech for the new Presbyterian Church. Judge W. D. Brown and Lieutenant Governor Charles W. Stone also delivered short speeches. History records that the church collection on dedication day came to $23.00.

In 1936, the congregation transferred to the Erie Presbytery from the Buffalo Presbytery. Records indicate that as late as the 1940s the Erie Presbytery gave $300 annually to its support. Reverend Paul G. Miller of the Bradford East End Presbyterian Church ministered. Miss Louise Gordon and Mrs. Harriett Bennett were elders of the church.

1885 Presbyterian Church, Cornplanter Grant.
Unidentified man with horse and buggy, Cornplanter Grant.

A quarter-century later these properties were put up for sale, as the valley was soon to be flooded with the waters of the Allegheny Reservoir. The church and its nearby mission house, property of Erie Presbytery, sold for $3,400 and $1,000 respectively. The brick schoolhouse, property of the Commonwealth of Pennsylvania, sold for $2,300. Mr. Victor Samuelson of Bradford, Pennsylvania, was the successful bidder at the December 18, 1964, sale. The land, on which the buildings stood, Cornplanter land, was valued by the state of Pennsylvania at $500. Plans for Kinzua Dam were moving ahead rapidly. Aside from the Cornplanters, the losses of the Seneca Reservation Indians needed to be addressed.

Senator Kenneth B. Keating, Republican, New York, October, 1964, in a speech to an audience at Chautauqua, New York, said: "The cost of breaking a U.S. treaty comes high, and it should come high. A treaty involving a few hundred Indians should be just as sacred as that involving millions."

The earliest known estimate of the number of Senecas in 1660 and 1677 placed them at about 5,000, inclusive of all locations. These are estimates made by knowledgeable Europeans, and recorded at that time. On June 30, 1962, there were 4,132 on the Seneca tribal rolls. There were 2,976 enrolled of the Seneca Nation residing on the Allegany and Cattaraugus reservations. On June 30, 1962, of the 922 members of Seneca families living on the Allegany Reservation, 482 (53%) resided in the reservoir taking area. At this time the population of the Cattaraugus Reservation was approximately 2,000. Exact population counts were difficult as people were often temporarily away from the reservation for employment.

It is highly noteworthy that the following statement appeared in the *1890 Report on Indians Taxed and not Taxed in the United States,* in the Eleventh Census of the United States. In an *Extra Census Bulletin* to the 1890 report the government affirmed the following regarding the Iroquois:

> Their small numbers, compared to the enormous country they occupied and the government they originated, with their deeds of daring, will always excite and surprise. Their league, tribal and individual characteristics, and personal strength of will, together with their great courage and prowess, account for their success in war and methods which brought comfort and peace.
>
> The Six Nations are to American Indian life what the Greeks and Romans in ancient history were to the nations bordering the Mediterranean. Their generalship in war was of the highest,

their civilization and cultivation, for their surroundings, the most advanced, and their economies of life the most applicable and fit of all the American race within the present boundaries of the United States and Canada.

One would be extremely hard pressed to find a more glowing report by any government on any people anywhere. Consider also that the 1890 census reported a population of 15,870 Indians in the League of Nations. There was no correct census of Indian populations until 1890, but in 1660 it was estimated that the League of Nations' population was at 11,000. In 1890 the total acreage of the Six Nations was 87,327.73 acres. The population of the Cornplanter Grant in 1890 was 98: 87 Senecas and 11 Onondagas. One white was reported to be living on the Grant.

Cornplanter's intentions regarding his land were that they never be abandoned by his heirs through neglect, or that the land be taken by any intentional acts of the government, state or federal. Cornplanter died in 1836—thirty-five years later his land was divided. A special act of the Pennsylvania State Legislature in 1871 partitioned the Grant for the six children of Cornplanter. One-sixth share of land was given to each of Cornplanter's three sons: Charles, William, and Henry; and one-sixth to the daughters: Esther, Polly, and Ja-wa-ioh.

Polly O'Bail Logan received her sixth share of her father's land, which amounted to 148 acres—the whole of Liberality Island, 62 acres, and 86 acres of Planters Field. In 1871, being well advanced in years, and Cornplanter's only living child, Polly made her will on September 6, which was then recorded at the Warren County Courthouse, Warren, Pennsylvania. Polly died shortly after making her will—October of 1871.

Solomon O'Bail was given 49 acres. Solomon's sisters, Lucy O'Bail Thompson of Cattauragus and Emily O'Bail Hotbread of Tonawanda, New York, were given shares equal to Solomon's. It was Solomon who, in 1866, petitioned the state legislature in Harrisburg to have the monument to his grandfather, Chief Cornplanter, erected on the Grant.

In 1871, the Pennsylvania State Legislature partitioned the remainder of the Grant among Cornplanter's heirs. This partitioning would have been reasonably straightforward, if all of Cornplanter's children had left wills with specific instruction regarding their land on the Cornplanter Grant, but only Polly had the forethought to do so. Ninety-four years later, the owners of this land needed to be identified and compensated by the U.S. Government, as these ancestral lands were soon to be flooded by the Kinzua Dam and the Allegheny Reservoir.

In July of 1965, Federal Judge Joseph P. Wilson took this perplexing case under advisement. The case had 250 petitioners—all eventually testified before

Judge Wilson. All 250 individuals awaited the judge's decision as to whether they were direct descendants of Chief Cornplanter. Among the petitioners were Martha Two Guns, Mary Steeprock, Hilton Henhawk, Lyman Warrior, Thalman Halftone and Clifford Red Eye.

All those legally proving direct kinship with Cornplanter would share the $75,000 the government eventually paid for the condemned Cornplanter Grant. Remember, this land case could have been easily settled if all the children of Cornplanter had left wills—they had not. Only Polly O'Bail Logan had left a will. Without a doubt, Judge Wilson needed the help of a team of genealogists. The state legislature partitioned the Grant for the six children in 1871, but after that everything slowly went haywire regarding *ownership* of the land—especially when the government wished to settle, in 1965, with the remaining owners of the original Cornplanter Grant.

Amidst all the details and dickering there is a remarkable story which surrounds an *outsider* who tried to wind up with some of the money from the federal government. Webster Lee of Salamanca, New York, claimed no kinship with Cornplanter, but produced an aged scrap of paper for the judge showing that in 1907 he had loaned one Harvey Jacobs $30 to buy a cow. Jacobs, dead in 1965, had put his land up as collateral for the borrowed $30. Jacobs had written the deal on a piece of paper in his own handwriting. It was then legally established that Harvey Jacobs was a legal heir to Cornplanter, and that the cow loan had not been repaid. Jacobs had no descendants. In 1965, Webster Lee aimed to collect about $3,000 on his $30 cow loan made in 1907 to Harvey Jacobs.

With the imminent flooding of the upper Allegheny River Valley, the relocation of ancestral burial grounds was an immense concern for the Seneca Indians. Non-economic forces, including intangible damages, are important elements in land taking by any government entity. These sometimes indefinable damages are often more crucial to the affected population than any strictly measured market terms and population counts. This is particularly true for burial grounds, which hold great spiritual significance—worth not measured by pragmatic or mere empirical means.

On August 13, 1964, the Grant Irwin Company of Honesdale was awarded a $343,782.37 contract by the U.S. Army Corps of Engineers for the relocation of 43 Indian cemeteries on the Allegany Reservation to two re-interment areas. The Indian cemeteries on the Allegany Reservation were below the 1,365-foot high water Allegheny Reservoir line, and they needed to be relocated above this maximum flooding elevation level. Indian burials from the Allegany Reservation were moved to two new Indian cemeteries in New York State, but none were moved to the Riverview Cemetery in Pennsylvania.

The two new national cemeteries were established by the Seneca Nation of Indians for relocation of graves from the 43 Allegany Reservation burial grounds. These cemeteries were to be *national* in terms of the Seneca Nation of Indians. Total size of the 43 burial areas was estimated at ten acres. Twenty-seven cemeteries containing 1,744 graves were relocated to Hillside Haven, Steamburg, New York. Steamburg is occasionally referred to as Cold Springs. Sixteen cemeteries with 1,260 graves were relocated to Memorial Heights, adjacent to Breed Run Road on Route 17, now Route 86, near Salamanca, New York.

Leo Cooper of Killbuck, New York, was employed by the U.S. Army Corps of Engineers as community liaison for cemetery relocations. Next of kin were to be located by a diligent search. Next of kin were to be given an opportunity to stipulate their re-interment preferences and their desire to be present during the move. How closely the U.S. Corps of Engineers followed these guidelines is difficult to determine.

All too often history indicates that perhaps the gravest harm imposed upon any governed people—in this case, American citizens, including American Indians—is the lessening of faith and conviction in the permanence of federal or state pledges and assurances; that is, durable treaties made in the best of faith by all. If treaties are made in earnest and kept without fail by both parties, then a trust of remarkable value is built among those involved—an example for all to view and follow. If that trust is violated, as in the breaking of the Treaty of 1794 by the U.S. Government, then unalterable damage is done to that highly valued trust—perhaps this is the gravest harm of all done to a people.

In the case of the Cornplanter Grant, owned as it was by heirs of Cornplanter and not a tribal government, and also in the case of the taken lands of the Allegany Reservation, reparation beyond mere real estate damages was non-existent—no procedure was established to recognize the intangible damages of a historical, religious, and cultural nature. This was beyond the scope of understanding of the U.S. Army Corps of Engineers, who were ill equipped to deal with the complexities of such a disturbance.

In 1963, Representative John P. Saylor (Pennsylvania), as a member of the Subcommittee on Indian Affairs of the Committee on Interior and Insular Affairs, House of Representatives, Eighty-Eighth Congress, spoke in no uncertain terms of the U.S. Army Corps of Engineers. The Corps had reported before this Congressional Committee that as of mid-1963 they had completed appraisals on 280 of the estimated 450 tracts of land in the Indian area—Seneca Reservation land. Too many impediments still remained in general planning—relocation of families, consideration of intangible damages, and rehabilitation to name a few. Simple things, such as the Seneca's reluctance to incur indebtedness on new homes when so many of the families previously owned their homes outright, were not understood. Representative Saylor's statement to representatives of the Corps of Engineers regarding their lack of completeness of property appraisals as late as 1963 follows:

> Certainly this *(the incomplete appraisals)* to me does not indicate that the Corps of Army Engineers has any respect for the President of the United States, for this committee *(Committee on Interior and Insular Affairs)*, or for the Congress, much less having any respect whatsoever for the members of the Indian tribe.
>
> To show you the disdain which the Army Engineers apparently have for this committee, at the front of both Mr. Hart's *(Loney W. Hart, Legislative Services Office, Chief of Engineers)* statement and the statement by Mr. Berge, *(Woodrow L. Berge, Acting Director of Real Estate, Office of the Chief of Engineers, Department of the Army)* it says that their statements are not to be released by the Committee of the House Public Works. They do not even know what committee they are appearing before.
>
> It is about time somebody with the Corps of Army Engineers finds out that this committee has tried over the years to deal gently with them, but apparently you don't understand that kind of dealing. Apparently you don't want to be treated nicely. Apparently you don't want to do anything for this Indian tribe. Apparently you have become so calloused and so crass that the breaking of the oldest treaty that the United States has is a matter of little concern to you, and the testimony we have had this morning, so far as I am concerned just adds evidence of the fact, showing that the Corps of Engineers has never intended to do anything whatsoever with regard to the Seneca Indians, and they have intended from the very beginning to treat this as just any other dam and leave the Indians their only recourse in the courts.
>
> Mr. Chairman, *(Wayne N. Aspinall, Colorado, Chairman)* I hope that this committee and the speaker will report out a bill which will be passed. I am assured by the White House it will be signed if we can get it through, and tell the Army Engineers that this is not an ordinary project. This is one which has the highest priority in the United States, and one which should call upon some people in the Corps of Army Engineers to pay some

consideration to the Department of the Interior, the Indian Bureau, and this committee.

Harsh words, indeed. Mr. Hart, Legislative Services Office, Chief of Engineers, in a statement of July 15, 1963, to the Committee, attempted to pass the entire blame for unconscionable foot-dragging in human planning onto the Bureau of Indian Affairs and the Seneca Nation of Indians. No passing of blame in planning could be wholly supported by the truth, but the truth could include one troublesome example of delay—the Corps of Engineers' failure to begin construction of urgently needed new roads, particularly residential roads.

Walter Taylor, a representative of the Seneca Nation of Indians from the Indian Committee of the Philadelphia Yearly Meeting of Friends (Quakers), exposed this crisis to the Subcommittee on Indian Affairs. In 1963, Taylor referenced one severe damage already suffered for years by Seneca families, on account of the Kinzua Dam, that was anxiety—apprehension of what to expect. Taylor continued. He explained that no homeowners in the *take area* could get enough information, even in late 1963, to relieve their worries about an uncertain future. One could not build a new home until new roads were ready, yet no roads were being built. If roads were not completed in time for the next year's (1964) construction of new homes, it would be necessary for Congress to delay the closing of the Kinzua Dam gates until "neglected human engineering catches up with so-called civil engineering," according to Taylor.

In early autumn of 1964, Seneca Nation leaders went into action to implement plans made possible by a House-Senate committee agreement on a $15 million settlement for losses due to Kinzua Dam. The figure represented a final compromise between the $20.15 million bill approved by the House in 1963 and the $9 million version passed by the Senate in the spring of 1964. The Senecas had requested $29 million for losses.

Replacement housing now became the critical priority for the 700 people on the Allegany Reservation whose homes were soon to be flooded. At this late date housing issues were still unresolved to the satisfaction of many Seneca—rightfully so, as the Army Corps of Engineers was reluctant to deal with the special needs of the Seneca Indians.

With insufficient housing plans projected to cause delays in the closing of the flood gates of the Kinzua Dam, work soon began on two relocation sites for displaced Senecas: one was at Jimersontown, New York, and the other site was at Steamburg (Cold Springs), New York.

Jimersontown, near Salamanca, New York, was laid out in 145 one-acre plots. Steamburg, near the southern end of the reservation, had 160 one-acre plots. A family could be eligible for as many as three plots, so each private homesite for a Seneca family could consist of up to three acres.

Also, there was a definite need to develop financially viable and profitable ventures for the new communities of Jimersontown and Steamburg. In a booklet entitled *The 1965 Challenge to Seneca Indians and to All Americans,* published by the Kinzua Project of the Indian Committee of the Philadelphia Meeting of Friends (Quakers), it states:

> The development of economic enterprise to ensure more and better jobs for members of the Nation will take more time, but planning is under way.

George Heron, administrator for the Seneca Nation of Indians at this time, elaborated on this point:

> Many families have needed little money to exist. They had their woodlots and with the wood they heated their home at no cost. They had their wells for water and grew food. Now they'll have gas and water bills. But we got enough acreage so there will be room for crops.

In 1960 when Mr. George Heron was President of the Seneca Nation of Indians, he made the following statement to the House Subcommittee on Indians Affairs regarding Seneca Indian relocation:

> The thought that we would freely give up the lands of our ancestors, which we are pledged to hold for our children yet unborn, is so contrary to the Seneca way of life that it is not even considered seriously…Now let me tell you a little bit about what the Kinzua Dam will do to my people. Our own census shows that over 700 members of the Nation, or more than half the population of the Allegany Reservation, will be forced to move by the reservoir. On paper, this does not seem like very many people; other lands, substitute houses can be found say the supporters of the project. If you knew these Senecas the way I do, though, if you knew how much they love that land—the last remnant of the original Seneca country—you would learn a different story. To lose their homes on the reservation is really to lose a part of their life.

The Corps of Engineers will tell you that Kinzua Dam will flood only 9,000 out of the 29,000 acres within the Allegany Reservation. What the Corps of Engineers does not say is that this 9,000 acres includes almost all the flat lowlands and fertile riverbanks, while the remainder of the Reservation is inaccessible and thus virtually uninhabitable mountainside. What the Corps also does not say is that during the dry season these 9,000 acres will not be a lake, but rather muck and mud flats. What a pleasant yearly reminder, what an annual memorial to the breaking of the 1794 Treaty that will be.

Educational needs were also addressed by the Seneca Nation of Indians. Roughly $12.2 million was allocated for rehabilitation, of which $1.8 million was to go to establish a precedent-setting educational scholarship fund for Indian young people. The fund was expected to be exhausted after twenty years; having anticipated sending 970 Senecas through college and 519 through vocational training. A board of trustees, with 5 Senecas, the heads of area school systems, a representative of the state, and the Bureau of Indian Affairs was to administer the program and determine eligibility. The hope was to fully educate an entire generation of Senecas, providing an improved standard of living for families that would allow them to educate themselves from there forward. The remaining funds were to be used for direct and indirect damages and administrative expenses.

The Indian land taking on the Allegany Reservation involved more than 700 parcels on some 10,000 acres. This was fully one-third of the Allegany Reservation. Well-established communities were destroyed, lives uprooted, and connections to places of birth severed. The lands taken had great religious and social significance to the Indians. They knew, in their hearts and minds, that their rights were trampled and lost. Reservation land taking had disturbing influences well beyond the Allegheny Reservoir area, to other stable, cohesive parts of the reservation and to Senecas not residing on the Allegany Reservation.

The right of eminent domain as declared by the government prevailed; the government took land and property from owners for what was determined as the greater good for the greater number of people. Kinzua Dam displaced people, towns, railroads, and highways. This is true of all dams, but Kinzua was complicated by a perpetual treaty signed by the League of Six Nations and the federal government.

The Senecas never chose to sell their land but the government was determined to take it. Removal and destruction of Seneca homes and lands was a direct violation of the Treaty of 1794. The signers of the oldest treaty to which the United

States is still a party, a treaty signed by George Washington, never envisioned a city such as Pittsburgh arising and clamoring for a system of dams as protection against floods and health-menacing pollution.

The cries of the whippoorwill echoed across the centuries.

After centuries of conflict and government treaties, it is a wonder that any lands remain for the Seneca to claim as their own. This is especially evident when surveying the remnants of the Cornplanter Grant, including Reservation Island.

Prior to the Allegheny Reservoir the total acreage of the mainland of the Cornplanter Grant, often referred to as Planters Field, was 784.12 acres. After inundation there are 164.82 acres above water and 619.30 acres below water. The remaining acreage borders the west side of the Allegheny Reservoir. It is approximately 3 miles from the New York–Pennsylvania State line and approximately nine miles upstream of the Kinzua Dam site. Land below water is land 1,365 feet above sea level or less, as the high water mark of the Allegheny Reservoir is 1,365 feet above sea level.

Reservation Island, now totally inundated, consisted of the two islands named in the original patents: Liberality and Donation. Reservation Island had a total acreage of 123.63 acres. After inundation there was no land above water.

The total of the mainland and island acreage was 907.75, with 164.82 total acres above water and 742.93 acres below water as a result of the Allegheny Reservoir. Map number 3 illustrates the Cornplanter Grant before and after inundation by the Allegheny Reservoir.

The residual land above water is divided by Cornplanter Run and is mostly inaccessible. It consists of steep hillsides and is best accessed by boat. The 742.93 acres below water essentially contains all the usable land and the improvements that had been completed on the Cornplanter Grant. These figures were obtained from the *Allegheny Reservoir Report on Cornplanter Grant in Elk Township, Warren County, Pennsylvania,* by the U.S. Army Corps of Engineers, Pittsburgh District, Pittsburgh, Pennsylvania, March, 1962.

The Cornplanter Grant was only one of three tracts of land that was bestowed upon Cornplanter for his services to the newly formed American government. The first land conferred was the Cornplanter Grant—as previously described: Planter's Field on the western bank of the Allegheny River, plus the two large river islands of Donation and Liberality. This tract included Jenuch-Shadega, the main settlement of Cornplanter and his people.

Other land granted to Cornplanter in 1791 included Richland and the Gift. Richland is near the present site of West Hickory in Forest County. Cornplanter promptly sold this land to his good friend, General John Wilkins, Jr. The Gift, the third land grant, is the present-day business district of Oil City, Pennsylvania.

Cornplanter wanted the Gift because it included an oil spring used by the Indians for medicinal purposes. This land was later sold by Cornplanter, in 1818, to William Connelly, of Venango County, and to William Kinnear, of Center County. The price was $2,120, with $250 to be paid in cash without delay. The rest of the debt was to be paid over a period of time. Cornplanter soon came to believe he had been swindled out of this land. Certain that he had been defrauded, Cornplanter created quite an uproar. The situation was never resolved to his satisfaction; he never forgot this loss, nor forgave those who cheated him. This rout was never forgotten by the heirs of Cornplanter either, and the idea that this land in the central business district of Oil City may again be theirs, has not been abandoned by some remaining Cornplanters today. There is an estimated 600 heirs of Chief Cornplanter. Most of these descendants are enrolled members of the Seneca Nation of Indians.

The Seneca Nation of Indians once *owned* all of the lands in western New York State and significant portions of the Commonwealth of Pennsylvania. Today the Seneca Nation has three reservations—all in western New York State.

The Allegany Indian Reservation is located along both sides of the Allegheny River, from the Pennsylvania border upriver to Vandalia, New York. It is entirely in Cattaraugus County and includes the City of Salamanca—the only city situated on an Indian Reservation. Originally the land totaled 30,469 acres, but some 10,000 acres of that total were inundated by the Allegheny Reservoir. The acres flooded were undoubtedly the most productive for agriculture, hunting, and fishing.

The second reservation is the Cattaraugus Indian Reservation. Its 21,680 acres are located in three counties of western New York State—the counties of Erie, Chautauqua, and Cattaraugus. These lands extend along the Cattaraugus Creek from Gowanda, New York, to Lake Erie.

The third reservation, the Oil Springs Reservation, is located in Cattaraugus and Allegany counties near Cuba, New York. Oil Springs encompasses a square mile of land, originally surveyed to protect the natural oil springs found there. These springs were used by the Seneca for medicinal purposes. No Seneca currently reside at the Oil Springs Reservation.

Other reservation lands where Senecas will be found are the lands allotted in the northeastern part of Oklahoma, where members of the Seneca-Cayuga Tribe of Oklahoma reside. There is also the Tonawanda Band of Seneca who occupy the Tonawanda Reservation. On this land, near Akron, New York, a tribal government by chiefs continues. They maintain a tribal membership roll separate from the other Seneca groups, and membership in the Iroquois Confederacy is maintained. An additional Seneca group resides on the Six Nations Reservation at Brantford, Ontario, Canada.

CORNPLANTERS

Lest we forget ~

"Mr. President!

"Where is the land upon which our children, and their children after them, are to lie down?"

"The merits of Cornplanter and his friendship for the United States are well known to me, and shall not be forgotten...."

(An exchange that occurred between Cornplanter and President George Washington in Philadelphia, Pennsylvania, 1790.)

The Seneca, a remarkable people by any measure, lay claim to many individuals of distinction and honor. Rudyard Kipling (1865-1936), as noted in *Stepping Stones, Vol.2, No.3, p.56,* a publication of the Warren County Historical Society, wrote admirably of Cornplanter, Red Jacket, and George Washington. They were regarded by Kipling as the three greatest persons in American life. The main characters of two stories in Kipling's *Rewards and Fairies* represent these men. It is also believed that the poem, *IF,* which appears between the two stories *Philadelphia* and *A Priest In Spite of Himself,* was inspired by these individuals.

The following verse is from *Philadelphia.*

> If you're off to Philadelphia this morning,
>> And wish to prove the truth of what I say,
> I pledge my word you'll find the pleasant land behind
>> Unaltered since *Red Jacket* rode that way.
> Still the pine-woods scent the noon; still the catbird sings his tune;
>> Still autumn sets the maple-forest blazing.
> Still the grape-vine through the dusk flings her soul-compelling musk;
>> Still the fire-flies in the corn make night amazing!
> They are there, there, there with Earth immortal
>> (Citizens, I give you friendly warning).
> The things that truly last when men and times have passed,
>> They are all in Pennsylvania this morning!

Chief Sagoyouwatha, also known as Red Jacket, was a Seneca orator and an eloquent spokesman for his people. Red Jacket did not agree with Cornplanter's cooperation with the emerging government of the United States and the selling of Indian land. In an address made in 1811 to a council of whites in New York State, Red Jacket explained:

> Your application for the purchase of our lands is to our minds very extraordinary. We are determined not to sell our lands but to continue on them....
>
> At the treaties held for the purchase of our lands, the white men, with sweet voices and smiling faces, told us they loved us, and

that they would not cheat us…these things puzzle our heads, and we believe that the Indians must take care of themselves, and not trust…in your people.

A few years after this address by Red Jacket, Cornplanter, too, became disillusioned with the treatment of his people by whites and the federal government. His outlook grew similar to that of Red Jacket. Loss of land over the years contributed significantly to changes in viewpoint.

Land has always been the very root of Indian existence and identity, and its loss—particularly ancestral burial lands—was traumatic to the spiritual heritage of the Cornplanter heirs—and to the integrity of the American government in their eyes.

Graves on the ancestral burial grounds had to be moved due to the Allegheny Reservoir. The archaeological study of the Cornplanter graves was conducted by two graduate students of the University of Buffalo, Audrey J. Sublett and George H. Abrams, under the direction of Dr. Marian E. White, associate professor of anthropology. When the remains of Chief Cornplanter were thought to be found, there were four Cornplanter Indians present, one of them an official liaison to supervise the removal of the graves, in addition to the anthropologists.

When Cornplanter's burial site was excavated, some expressed concern that no jewelry or medals were found in his casket, as a ceremonial burial had been expected. Merle Deardorff, friend of the Indians and local historian well versed in Indian lore and culture, noted that by 1818 Cornplanter had destroyed all his medals, everything the Americans had given him. By this time Cornplanter had rejected his alliance of many years with the white man. He had become disillusioned with state and federal government; therefore, no symbols that could represent this previously trusted friendship were to be found in his burial site.

Cornplanter Cemetery, located in its entirety within the Cornplanter Grant, contained 358 graves, as determined by inspection and surveys by the U.S. Army Corps of Engineers. It was approximately one acre in size. The best known breakdown of excavations at the Cornplanter Grant indicated 115 graves containing bones, 129 with other artifacts, and 358 total excavations. It is thought that only descendants of Cornplanter were allowed to be buried in the cemetery. All of the bodies had been buried with their heads to the west.

Dr. White of the University of Buffalo said many observations were made hurriedly because the contractor was moving up to 60 graves a day to the new site for re-burial. In order to make any close observations and measurements, the anthropologists strived to receive the consent of the next of kin when known. In no way could a thorough and methodical study of the sites be accomplished when 60 graves a day were moved. At this pace how careful and complete could the re-interment process have been, aside from accomplishing any interpretive anthropological study of the remains?

According to U.S. Army Corps of Engineer plans, all graves from the cemetery at the Cornplanter Grant were to be moved to the Riverview Cemetery across the Allegheny River. (*See Map 4.*) The Cornplanter Cemetery was determined to be a separate area within the larger Riverview Cemetery. The Cornplanter area at the present cemetery has a 12-foot-wide roadway around the entire perimeter. It is approximately 1.6 acres in size and provides for 695 burials.

The average mean sea level at the original Cornplanter Cemetery on the Grant was 1,255 feet above sea level, well below the Allegheny Reservoir high water mark of 1,365 feet above sea level. At high water, the old Cornplanter Cemetery on the Grant is under 110 feet of Allegheny Reservoir water. To this day, some descendants of Cornplanter wonder just how many bones were left behind, and are to be found far under the dark Allegheny water, locked forever in the silt of the valley floor.

Chief Cornplanter's original burial place on the Grant.
This was the first monument ever erected to memorialize
an Indian Chief by any State in the Union. The monument
was erected October 18, 1866.   c.1955.

The first monument ever erected to memorialize an Indian Chief by any State in the Union was erected to Chief Cornplanter at his original burial place on the Grant. This monument was accomplished by a special act of the General Assembly of Pennsylvania in 1866. On October 18, 1866, Cornplanter's three sons were present when the monument was unveiled. In 1871 the area around the monument on the Grant was partitioned as a burial ground. At this time there were nearly 100 members of the family living on the Grant.

The original inscriptions on the monument to Cornplanter were cut by hand with a chisel and were quite shallow; time and weather took their toll. The monument had been taken apart and the lettering partially restored, again with a hand chisel, in 1954, ten years before it was moved from its original location on the Cornplanter Grant to the Riverview Cemetery in 1964. With the impending flooding of the Grant, the relocation of the Cornplanter Monument was a high priority with the Senecas.

In November, 1977, the historic monument to Chief Cornplanter, now relocated to Riverview Cemetery overlooking the Allegheny Reservoir, was again cleaned and restored. The most noticeable work done was in the restoration of the lettering, which had been defaced by natural erosion of the stone. The renewed lettering was cut as deep as half an inch with sandblasting. Messerly Monument Works of Warren, Pennsylvania, did the work.

The inscription upon the north side of the monument reads:

GY-ANT-WA-HIA, THE CORNPLANTER
JOHN O'BAIL, ALIAS CORNPLANTER
DIED AT CORNPLANTER TOWN,
FEB. 18, A.D. 1836
AGED ABOUT 100 YEARS

The west side inscription reads:

Chief of the Seneca Tribe, and a principal Chief of the Six Nations, from the period of the Revolutionary War to the time of his death. Distinguished for talents, courage, eloquence and sobriety, and love of his tribe and race, to whose welfare he devoted his time, his energies and his means, during a long and eventful life.

The east side inscription reads:

> Erected by Authority of the Legislature of Pennsylvania. By Act
> passed March A.D. 1866.

Cornplanter having lived a century long is questionable. Recent research
(*Cornplanter*, Swatzler) indicates that Cornplanter was most likely born 1750-
1752, not the 1736 as indicated on his monument.

In 1998, the 1866 monument was removed from Riverview Cemetery. The
new monument, very near in likeness, was placed in the Cornplanter–Seneca
Cemetery within the Riverview Cemetery. It was delivered to the Riverview site
by a crew from O'Rourke Monument Company in Salamanca, New York. On
Sunday, October 18, 1998, 132 years after the original monument dedication on
the Cornplanter Grant, the new monument was unveiled.

The original monument was made of Vermont marble, frequently used for
head stones in the 18th and 19th centuries because of the ease with which it could
be cut by hand. Monument makers now generally use Barre granite, which is
much harder than marble and much less subject to erosion. Granite erodes very
slowly, reportedly only about 1 millimeter every thousand years.

The 1998 replica, being somewhat less ornate than the original, was made of
granite. It bears three inscriptions from the original monument and the fourth
side which was blank on the original, denotes the good deed of the Chief
Cornplanter Council, Boy Scouts of America, for their help in organizing the
monument replication project.

A $25,000 Department of Community and Economic Development grant
was obtained to purchase the replica and to provide for cleaning and refurbishing
of the original monument. The 1866 monument was to be displayed in the
Seneca-Iroquois National Museum in Salamanca, New York. Duwayne "Duce"
Bowen, past president of the Seneca Nation of Indians, was chairman of the
Cornplanter Monument Committee. The weathered monument did not end up
in the museum as originally planned. The weight of the 3-ton monument made
it impossible to put it inside the existing Seneca Nation museum in Salamanca—
the structure could not accommodate it. Today it is in storage in Salamanca,
reportedly awaiting refurbishment.

An image of three of Cornplanter's children follows. The men are Charles
O'Bail and William O'Bail. The woman, in all probability, is Polly O'Bail,
though her identity is not entirely certain. Charles was born circa 1780, and died
before 1871; William, born circa 1786, also died before 1871; and Polly O'Bail,
born 1783, died October, 1871. Not shown are Henry O'Bail, born circa 1778,
died before 1836; Esther O'Bail, who married Moses Pierce; and Ja-wa-ioh, who
married Abraham Silverheels. Birth and death dates of Esther and Ja-wa-ioh are
indeterminate. Solomon O'Bail, 1814–1899, was a grandson of Cornplanter.

Charles O'Bail   William O'Bail

Polly O'Bail

Solomon O'Bail, grandson of Cornplanter.

Another noteworthy Seneca personage was Louis Bennett, commonly known as Deerfoot. At the time of the Warren Centennial, 1895, Deerfoot came to town as a guest of honor on a special train from the Cattaraugus Reservation in New York State. He was 65 years old at that time and the holder of several unbroken world records in long-distance running. He raced on many of the notable tracks in the United States and on all the important tracks in Europe. He was never beaten in a race.

Deerfoot was born on the Cattaraugus Reservation around 1830, the son of a notable Seneca family. In 1856 he entered a race at the Fredonia, New York, fairground where he ran five miles in twenty-five minutes to win a prize of $50. Later in 1856 he raced at Buffalo, New York, where he ran ten miles in 58 minutes to win $40. From this time on, he raced wherever he could and became known as *the man to beat* among those in the know.

In 1861, George Martin, an Englishman and trainer of long-distance runners, came to the United States specifically to see Deerfoot run. Martin persuaded Deerfoot to return with him to England. Martin matched him against the great James Putney, the long-distance champion of England, for a ten-mile challenge. Putney, having heard of Deerfoot's accomplishments, failed to show, and the championship was awarded to Deerfoot.

On April 3, 1863, Deerfoot raced in London, England. He ran eleven miles on this day in just 52 minutes and 52 seconds. The crowds cheered and adored him. Deerfoot became homesick and soon after this event returned home to America. Although appearing somewhat aged at 65, when he appeared at the Warren Centennial in 1895, no one could ever question the vitality and abilities of this remarkable man. Shortly after the Centennial, Deerfoot died and was buried on the Cattaraugus Reservation.

Louis Bennett, also known as Deerfoot.

This image was published in London, 1861.

Cornplanter Indians seine fishing, Allegheny River, c. 1940.

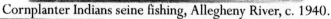

Wellman Bowen, Cornplanter Indian, working the ferry on the Allegheny River, near the Cornplanter Grant. c. 1930.

Below, Phoebe Gordon weaving Seneca baskets. c. 1915-1920.

It is no wonder that few people were ever aware of the existence of the Cornplanter Indians—or of their specific whereabouts—for their grant of land was almost inaccessible in terms of modern transportation. When the great-grandson of Cornplanter, Ezra Jacobs, died, it was necessary for the state of Pennsylvania to do a quick repair job on the road that followed the Allegheny River to Corydon. Ezra Jacobs, who was a Chief of the Cornplanters, had served in the Spanish-American War. After fellow members of the Warren Veterans of Foreign Wars provided an ordinary Christian burial service for him, Ezra was to be transported by hearse to his ancestral burial grounds.

The road that led to the Grant was a narrow, twisting, 16-mile lane that led from Highway 6, a mile east of Warren, Pennsylvania, to the Corydon side of the Allegheny River. The road was dangerous in summer and virtually impassable in winter. Today this road, Route 59—even with rebuilding and relocation due to Kinzua Dam and the Allegheny Reservoir, as well as the availability of modern road building equipment—still seems to be in need of regular repair. After the procession arrived at a location somewhat south of Corydon, attendees still needed to cross the Allegheny River, via ferry, to arrive at the burial site on the Grant.

Only a few people made the trip into the Grant for the burial, as the road was in such terrible repair. Others did not cross the Allegheny River. They watched from the east bank, directly across from the Cornplanter Grant.

In 1952 Miss Lucia E. Browne, school teacher, offered these comments on road maintenance:

> The state provides $600 every two years for road work. That's not a drop in the bucket…I've seen twenty-five good two-story houses rot and fall apart. The Indians use to till the land and everyone had a cow, chickens, and a pig. Now there is hardly one garden plot.

Roads and land transportation were so bad that some just ignored the road out of the Grant for most of the year. Miss Lucia E. Browne—who by Thanksgiving Day had stocked up sufficient food and other necessities to last over until spring, when the road again was passable—was a prime example.

Residents and some visitors did cross over the Allegheny River by boat or barge to get in and out of the Grant. In deep winter, when the river was frozen over, it was possible to walk across. This inaccessibility caused some Indians to move away from the Grant because they could earn a living more easily and live more comfortably elsewhere. Houses and gardens were slowly, but surely, abandoned.

Bit by bit, the Commonwealth of Pennsylvania lost interest in the future of the Cornplanter Indians. Transportation improved all around, but the river remained almost the sole means for the Cornplanters to maintain contact with other settlements. Even the Seneca lands to the north, reservation land, had improved routes of transportation, as they were bisected with modern highways. Opportunities to earn a livelihood are generally more available when better transportation is available. These opportunities were denied the Cornplanters who had no access to them.

Many Cornplanters today reside in New York State where they are influential citizens. These same individuals maintain sentimental attachments to their Pennsylvania homelands. On occasion, some return for a visit to the remaining Cornplanter acres along the Allegheny Reservoir.

A major event on the Cornplanter Grant was the adoption of Pennsylvania Governor Arthur H. James, August 24, 1940, by the Seneca Nation of Indians. This was one of the last historic events on the Cornplanter Grant by the Seneca people. Attendance at the Governor's Adoption Ceremony was approximately 3,000 people.

Windsor Pierce was the Governor's sponsor, as well as the oldest living direct descendant of Cornplanter at the time. Alice White, clan mother of Governor James, was the oldest woman of the Wolf Clan. Her Seneca name was Gyhn-Dah-Qua, meaning "She Picks Up Plants."

After a full day's deliberation, Alice White and other clan women selected the new Seneca name for the governor. Names are clan property and only the clan mother may give names to individuals. Originally, in Iroquois tradition, every name had its own wampum strand which was placed over the head of the recipient and reclaimed upon his death.

Na-Neng-Geh Hey-Geh-Owa-Ah-Na-Gwah Na-Wan-Nes-Ha-Deh,
Neh Deg-Yoh-Wa-Dont-Tah Wen-Nee-Da-Deh Joh-Doh-Sky,
Nee-Went-Yah-A Gayee-Sky-Nee-Yos-Nes-Heh Wa-Dont-Ta,
Na-Yos-Had-Da. Neh DOE-NOH-GO-WAS Ten-Nuh-Doh
The HONORABLE ARTHUR H. JAMES

Oh-Nung-Daw-Geh Neh Ho-A-We-Yus-Stoh Ho-Dey-Hud-Daw-Yeh.
Wah-Wa-Yong-Gweh-Daung-Goh., Neh Hah-De-Non-Doe-Wah-Oaw,
Wah-Wn-Yoh-Dun-Deh, HO-DE-TIE-YON-NEE NOH-DE-SAY-OH-DEH,
Wah-Woh-San-Noo, Wah-Woh-San-Nuh; O-DÄHN-OOHT Ha-Yaws-Soh,

Neng-ko Heh-o-Weh Neh Oniänt'wakä
Hah-Non-Dah-Gaw-Yos-Heh Diono sade'gi. Ang-Yen-Gwn Neh
Gnnowoñ-go' "NEH-HO-A-WE-YUS-STOH HO-DE-Y-HUD-DAW-YEH."

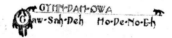

GYHN-DAH-OWA
Gaw-Sah-Deh Ho-De-No-Eh

Adoption ceremony scroll lettered in Seneca, above.

Pennsylvania Governor Arthur H. James, August 24, 1940, being adopted by the Seneca Nation of Indians, below.

A scroll lettered in Seneca by the noted Seneca artist, Sanford Plummer, of Gowanda, New York, was presented to the Governor. The picture at the top of the scroll is an Indian greeting a white man dressed in Quaker garb, symbolizing the Seneca's reception of William Penn's successor.

English translation of the scroll:

"On the afternoon of the 8th month, the 24th day,
1940th year, the Honorable Arthur H. James was
adopted by the Seneca as a member of the Wolf
Clan and given the name 'O-Dahn-Goht' meaning
'Sunlight', at Cornplanters old town of Diono-sade-gi,
in Warren County, Pennsylvania."

(Signed by)
Gyhn-Dah-Qua (She Picks Up Plants) Clan Mother.

On behalf of the Pennsylvania Federation of Historical Societies, a large colored portrait of Chief Cornplanter was presented to the children of the school at the Adoption Ceremony. The portrait was made from the original painting, now owned by the New York State Historical Society. The original, said to be the first American oil portrait of an Indian, was painted from life in 1796, by F. Bartoli. The children accepted the portrait and gave O-Dahn-Goht, Governor James, a box of ground berries.

On behalf of the Pennsylvania Federation of Historical Societies, a large colored portrait of Chief Cornplanter was presented to the children of the Cornplanter School at the adoption ceremony.

The Adoption Ceremony was also attended by Dr. Parker, Ga-wa-so-wan-neh, who was director of the Rochester Municipal Museum and a New York State archaeologist. Dr. Parker was a Seneca and grand-nephew of Seneca Major-General Ely Parker of the Civil War. Dr. Parker, who was related to many of the Cornplanter heirs, explained the great importance of the Adoption Ceremony in Indian ritual:

> Ritual to the red man is as natural as the rhythm of his breathing. It is his vicarious poetry and it characterizes his every ceremony. Thus, on this occasion the rite of adoption is to be exemplified, for a name is to be bestowed upon a man whose singular position commands attention and respect.
>
> Before the name can be given, however, certain invocations must be made, certain formalities must be gone through and there must be a public announcement sealed by the ceremonies of the Ostowah-gowa, for then the wind of the worlds is open and the spirits of things unseen will hear the name and remember it…And here let me mention one important characteristic of the old Long House League. It was established by the ancient fathers to emphasize responsibility.
>
> The Indian did not caterwaul in the night or stand upon soap boxes demanding, *I want my rights*. Instead, he loudly demanded that he be allowed to assume his responsibility. Nor did he ever demand that his government give him anything; it was he who wanted to give his government everything. He existed to give and not to get. And if the white man exploited that characteristic trait, it has been to the doom of the white man who, in America, I sadly fear, has cried for rights forgetting that every right received must be paid for with a service given; that for every right demanded a responsibility commensurate must be assumed. But the Long House with its political and social philosophy we consider as of no force in America today. Yet, should we not remember its tenets and acknowledge their value to us?

Dr. Parker's speech was especially poignant, as the historical importance of the Cornplanter Grant and its people has often gone unacknowledged. Many decisions affecting the Seneca Nation, the Iroquois Confederacy, and the development of the newly emerging United States of America were associated with

Cornplanter, his people, and the Grant. Dr. Parker said that square foot for square foot there is no more historically significant piece of land for the early development of this nation than the 907 acres of the Grant given to Cornplanter by the Commonwealth of Pennsylvania for his invaluable service to the young and struggling United States.

A further claim to fame of this historical land is the half-brother of Cornplanter, Handsome Lake. He had his visions of the Four Prophets while on the Grant, the first vision occurring in June of 1799. These visions led to the establishment of the Longhouse Religion—the Code of Handsome Lake—which still permeates segments of Iroquois life today.

Handsome Lake, in 1802, visited President Thomas Jefferson and returned with Jefferson's written endorsement of his *Good Message*. This set of new religious beliefs and practices has been described as a blending of traditional Seneca beliefs with an ethical code borrowed from the Quakers. The birth of the *Good Message* on this land endowed the Grant with even greater significance to the Cornplanters.

President Jefferson, in 1802, also received a visit from Cornplanter. Jefferson, in a statement nearly identical to President Washington's words on the security of Seneca lands, wrote the following in a letter issued by the War Department to the Seneca and Onondaga Nations on March 17, 1802.

> …All lands claimed and secured to said Seneca and Onondaga Nations of Indians by treaty, convention or deed of conveyance or reservation lying and being within the limits of the said United States, shall be and remain the property of the said Seneca and Onondaga Nation of Indians forever, unless they voluntarily relinquish or dispose of the same. All persons, citizens of the United States, are hereby strictly forbidden to disturb said Indian Nations in the quiet possession of said lands….

Both Washington and Jefferson were confronted with many critical problems, but both considered that no United States obligation was more solemn, or more demanding of their thoughtful consideration as President, than the Treaty of 1794. At that time Chief Cornplanter and the Seneca had assured the struggling new government of the United States of their support, when they were being encouraged by foreign powers to harass the United States and to thwart westward expansion by pioneers and settlers. For many, Indians and non-Indians alike, the unilateral abrogation of the Treaty of 1794 by the United States construction of the Kinzua Dam and the Allegheny Reservoir soured recollections of their

American legacy and heritage—promises made to last *as long as the grass shall grow.*

The last picnic on the Cornplanter Grant was August 3, 1964, as heirs to Cornplanter and their friends gathered on the ancestral land. The oldest and youngest heirs to Cornplanter were present at the event—Melody Thompson, six months, and Ray Bennett, 68 years of age. There was a unity at the gathering, as all present had the interest of the Cornplanters at heart.

Some at the last picnic were bitter, as expressed by Cornelius Seneca. He had lost faith in the government, both federal and local, due to the numerous times that the government had broken faith with the Indians.

Cornelius Seneca said:

> On this sacred ground the army burned up our homes. The Indians fled across the river to Cornplanter Mountain and watched their homes go up in smoke. Today we are not going up in smoke, but under water.

Many people thought that in the interest of *progress* the Kinzua Dam was necessary; that the Indians were compensated fairly for the land they lost; and that they were adequately assisted by the government with relocation problems—to the Indians the situation seemed immensely different. They were on the continent first and they did have what was considered to be an unbreakable treaty, the Treaty of 1794. The Seneca had felt secure in continuing in the ways of their heritage on land which was permanently theirs—poles apart from the *progress* many associated with Kinzua Dam. At the last picnic, Seneca President George Heron, said that the transition to the new life would not be an easy one for many.

> The younger people may not find it so difficult, but the older ones will find it hard. I know the feelings of the Indian people for their land. It's a part of their life.

The driving of Indians from their land began with the first ingress of white men into Indian Territory. With groundbreaking by the first pioneers and settlers, perhaps this opening of Indian land to outsiders occurred without major problems, but as white populations increased, the fight to maintain Indian land rights and lifestyle grew fiercely. In today's world when a struggle appears most hopeless, it is brought to the forefront by a celebrity with a conscience—such was the case with Johnny Cash.

In June, 1966, country-western singer Johnny Cash was adopted by the Seneca Nation of Indians. The adoption was a tribute for his 1964 recording, *As Long as the Grass Shall Grow.* The song tells of broken treaties and promises to Cornplanter and Seneca Indians when land was taken for construction of Kinzua Dam. Peter LaFarge, Indian friend of Cash, wrote the protest song, which is featured in the Cash recording titled *Bitter Tears.*

As long as the moon shall rise
As long as the rivers flow
As long as the sun will shine
As long as the grass shall grow

The Seneca are an Indian Tribe of the Iroquois Nation,
Down on the New York-Pennsylvania line you will find their reservation.
After the U.S. Revolution, Cornplanter was the Chief,
He told the tribe these men could be trusted. That was his true belief.
He went down to Independence Hall and a treaty was signed,
That promised peace to the U.S. and Indian rights combined.

George Washington gave his signature,
The Government gave its hand,
They said for now and evermore that this was Indian Land.

As long as the moon shall rise
As long as the rivers flow
As long as the sun will shine
As long as the grass shall grow

On the Seneca Reservation there is much sadness now,
Washington's treaty has been broken and there ain't no hope no how.

Across the Allegheny River they are putting up a Dam,
That will flood the Indian Country, a proud day for Uncle Sam.
It has broken an ancient treaty with a politician's grin,
It will flood the Indian's grave yards. Cornplanter can you swim?
The Earth is Mother to the Seneca, they have trampled sacred ground,
Changing the mint green earth to black mud flats hobble down.

As long as the moon shall rise
As long as the rivers flow
As long as the sun will shine
As long as the grass shall grow

The Iroquois Indians used to rule from Canada way south,
But no one fears the Indians now and smiles from a liars mouth.
The Seneca's hired an expert, to find another site,
But the wonderful Corps of Engineers said that they had no right.
Although he showed them another way, they laughed in his face,
And said KINZUA DAM IS HERE TO STAY!
Congress turned the Indians down, brushed away their plea,
So the Seneca has renamed the Dam, they call it LAKE PER-FIDY!

As long as the moon shall rise
As long as the rivers flow
As long as the sun will shine
As long as the grass shall grow

Washington, Adams and Kennedy now hear their pledges ring,
The treaty's safe we will keep our word. But what is that I hear gurgling?

It's the back waters from Lake Perfidy.

It's rising all the time, over the homes and fields, over the promise find,

No boats will sail over Lake Perfidy, and the winter it will fill.

In the Summer it will be a swamp, and all the fish it will kill,

But the Government of the USA has corrected George's Vow.

The father of our country must be wrong,

What's an Indian any how?

As long as the moon shall rise

As long as the rivers flow

As long as the sun will shine

As long as the grass shall grow

Johnny Cash always wore black—he often said, *for the beaten and the trodden down.* Cash had vowed not to wear anything but black until the Cornplanter Indians see their land returned. Johnny Cash, beloved and respected by many, passed away in 2003—still wearing black.

In 1966, during the Adoption Ceremony, Johnny Cash was named Ha-gao-ta, which means "Story Teller." Mrs. Nettie Watt of the Turtle Clan of the Senecas, his adoptive mother, gave Cash moccasins made of corn stalks. Mrs. Watt was one of the members of the Allegany Seneca Reservation who resettled in Salamanca, as a result of the dam construction.

Chief Corbett Sundown of the Tonawanda Seneca, Hawk Clan, conducted the adoption ceremonies. During an Indian chant, Cash was confirmed by four persons representing the four directions. Then several members of the tribe led him in two dances; one representing peace and the other a hunting expedition. Cash was one-quarter Cherokee Indian; his paternal grandmother was full-blood Cherokee.

It is a fact that no understanding of present-day Kinzua Dam, and the lands of the Allegheny and Ohio River Basin, can be complete without acknowledgement of the indelible imprint of the Seneca Nation on this region. The historical importance of these people has often gone unappreciated; their losses and sacrifices forgotten.

During the turbulent times through which he lived, it was Cornplanter's intelligent and far-seeing leadership that prevented the Seneca from sharing the fate of many Indians. For decades he knew that accommodations to the ways of the whites would prove necessary for the survival of the Seneca, though in his later years he reviled betrayals made by the government. Handsome Lake unquestionably determined the Seneca's ability to absorb some outside philosophy without discarding the basic foundation of Iroquois ideology—a significant survival tool and a tribute to the wisdom of the Cornplanter Indians and the Senecas.

Some refused to adjust. Red Jacket, the Seneca orator, rejected making accommodations to the ways of the whites. This he made evident in an 1829 speech.

> Brothers, as soon as the war with Great Britain was over, the United States began to part the Indians' land among themselves…permit me to kneel down and beseech you to let us remain on our own land—have a little patience—the Great Spirit is removing us out of your way very fast; wait a little while and we shall all be dead! Then you can get the Indians' land for nothing—nobody will be here to dispute it with you.

This speech was full of desperation and grim humor, but there is no denying that throughout the Americas, American Indian communities have been systematically deprived of their lands—a process begun shortly after the arrival of Europeans and continuing today.

FLOODS AS LIVELIHOOD

The years teach much which the days never knew.

~ Ralph Waldo Emerson

During the 19th century the Allegheny River was used primarily for navigation, which included exploration, settlement, trade, and commerce. Logging and farming were the major means of making a livelihood along the Allegheny River and its rich bottomlands. The Allegheny River and its major tributaries were the means to get the goods, primarily lumber, to market. Rafting lumber on the Allegheny River lasted from roughly 1800 to the early 1900s, just over a hundred years of high adventure.

The men who rode these lumber rafts bound for downriver markets made an adventurous and hardy crew. These river rafts of lumber were huge and unwieldy, and only accomplished rivermen were able to manage them during the brief high water times of spring. Rafting was an early spring occupation that coincided with the floods. Floods lasted 3 to 6 weeks, when the river carried a sufficient volume of water to float the lumber. The rest of the year the lumbermen prepared the trees for the following year's excursion.

These spring floods, vitally significant, provided the sole means of transport to market for a product from which many woodsmen earned their living—lumber. Any human intervention that eliminated these naturally occurring periods of high waters compromised navigation on the river by traditional means. *In essence, floods were the critical element in the livelihood of the woodsmen and rivermen.*

The market for lumber from the upper valleys of the Allegheny River was Pittsburgh, Pennsylvania, and points further downriver. This lumber would often begin its journey on a large tributary of the upper Allegheny, such as the Conewango Creek which enters the Allegheny at Warren, Pennsylvania. The size of the rafts would grow incrementally as they approached their destination.

Lumber raft passing under the lower railroad bridge, Warren. Below, early Hickory Street suspension bridge construction, with lumber rafts waiting for higher water on the Allegheny.

A great deal of information about the size of these river rafts and the number of men it took to *steer* them downriver to market was recorded in a January 16, 1926, letter from Harold Chase Putnam to his cousin, Aline Lewis, later Aline Burgett. Mr. Putnam, a Warren County historian and lifelong resident, visited his grandfather, Charles Chase, in Russell, Pennsylvania, a village on the Conewango Creek, to obtain the facts, figures, and river lore. The following historical details were gleaned directly from this letter to Aline Lewis and are particularly relevant, as Charles Chase, an accomplished riverman of his time, genuinely knew of what he spoke. *(Some data in the original letter has been converted from lists to paragraphs—all details remain exact, with a few comments added for clarity.)*

Only close to the streams was any timber cut in the summer; nearly all timber was cut in autumn and winter, when the sap had retreated and the logs could be handled on sleds. The logs were grouped in skid piles ready to be skidded onto sleds and hauled to the lumber mills. Originally all the mills were located on streams where water power was available, which necessitated hauling some of the logs a long-distance. When steam power was introduced, the mills were located in the woods near the cutting operations. The sawed lumber was hauled on sleds to the creek or river and there *rafted*. The gangs of lumbermen usually spent the winter in the woods near their work, living in shanties, or sometimes boarding with a jobber who had built a house in the woods.

During the three to six weeks of available rafting in the spring, all available space in the local taverns, including bar-room and ball-room, as well as the barn floors, was used as sleeping quarters by the waiting hands, eager to ride the rafts and take the lumber to market. Most of the waking hours were filled with feverish activity, owing to the necessity of taking advantage of the fleeting high water. It can easily be imagined that many of the rough and ready rivermen, primed with whiskey abundantly available at three cents a glass, found time to indulge in fights and wrestling matches. Many played High-Low-Jack, the popular card game of the time. Of course, there was no time for dances or other lingering and tame festivities.

Russell, Pennsylvania, then called Russellsburg, Russellburg, or Pine Grove, was the busiest and most important point on the Conewango Creek above Warren, Pennsylvania, during the rafting season because of the fact that it was at this point that the seven miles of rapids to Warren began. Russell is located north of Warren, Pennsylvania, and is approximately 15 miles due west of the Cornplanter Grant in Warren County.

In the slack water above Russell, no pilots were needed to conduct the lumber rafts downstream; below Russell, however, skillful handling was needed, due to the combination of the crooked stream, islands, and swift current. The number of pilots available, nearly all of whom dwelt in and around Russell, was limited, and for this reason during the spring, rafts practically covered the surface of the Conewango Creek for two miles above Russell, awaiting their turn to be piloted over the dam and on to Warren, there to be coupled into Alleghenys.

When a raft began its journey upriver from Russell, Pennsylvania, on the Conewango Creek, it required four men to handle it. This same raft, a Conewango Raft, traveling from Russell downstream to Warren and the confluence of the Allegheny River, required four men and a pilot.

Eventually Conewango Rafts were joined up to make Allegheny Rafts, and the crew grew to twelve hands, a pilot, and a cook. When Allegheny Rafts were joined to make Ohio Rafts, the crew again grew; fourteen to seventeen hands, a pilot, and a cook.

A Conewango Raft was ten 16-foot platforms long and one wide; dimensions approximately 16 ½ feet wide by 152 feet long.

Allegheny Rafts when made up of Conewango Rafts were 3 Conewango Rafts wide and 2 Conewango Rafts long; dimensions approximately 49 ½ feet wide and 304 feet long. Such an Allegheny Raft would contain six Conewango Rafts.

If the trip from Russell, Pennsylvania, were to a market past Pittsburgh an Ohio Raft was built. An Ohio Raft, when made up of Allegheny Rafts, which had been made from Conewango Rafts, was 2 Alleghenies wide and 1 ½ Alleghenies long for a total of 3 Alleghenies.

Allegheny Rafts when made up of Conewango Rafts were
3 Conewangos wide and 2 Conewangos long; dimensions
approximately 49 ½ feet wide and 304 feet long. The raft
above is only 2 Conewangos wide, but still its size is immense.
Below, a raft is tied up near a mill in Pittsburgh, Pennsylvania.

Conewango Rafts, Allegheny Rafts, and Ohio Rafts made up of Conewango units, were not as deep as rafts made up on the Allegheny itself, owing to the comparative shallowness of the Conewango. Rafts made up in the Allegheny River and not originating from a tributary, such as the Conewango Creek, were by nature larger.

These larger Allegheny River rafts were composed of units of six platforms, instead of five, as in the case of those coming from the Conewango Creek. They were 24 platforms long and three wide, with overall dimensions approximately 51 x 364 feet. At Pittsburgh two of these Alleghenies were coupled together side by side and a third cut in two and the two halves added to the end of the new raft, making the Ohio Raft 36 platforms long and six wide, the total width being 102 feet and the length approximately 540 feet.

One of these Ohio Rafts would cover over an acre of water and would contain from 1,200,000 to 1,300,000 feet of lumber. The number of courses, or layers of boards in the platforms, would be from 25 to 30, depending on whether the lumber was dry and light, in which case there could be more courses, or green and heavy, when the thickness of the raft would have to be less, in order that the draft be not excessive. These rafts ordinarily drew about 2 1/2 feet of water and rose above the water line about two feet.

The rafts were steered with immense oars. A Conewango Raft had one oar on each end; an Allegheny Raft, 3 oars on each end; an Ohio Raft, 6 oars on each end. In other words, there was one oar to each string, on each end of the raft, making a total of two oars on a Conewango Raft, 6 on an Allegheny, twelve on an Ohio.

In the early days the pay of a hand from Warren to Pittsburgh was $8.00 to $12.00, from Warren to Cincinnati, $30.00 to $35.00. Later on Charles Chase paid hands $45.00 to $50.00 for a trip from Warren to Louisville, Kentucky. A jobber, such as Charles Chase, was paid $3.10 a thousand feet of lumber for getting out the lumber, rafting it in, paying wages, furnishing supplies, and delivering the rafts at Louisville.

Once at their destination the crews had to make their way home. Raftsmen who went no farther than Pittsburgh usually walked all of the way home, a journey of four days, by way of Butler, Harrisville, Franklin, Enterprise, Torpedo, Garland, and Youngsville. The men would stop at taverns and log houses, which they happened to reach at dark. Occasionally the trip would be made by stagecoach, in whole or in part, or by steamboat to Emlenton, Franklin, Warren, or some other town, depending on whether the stage of water were favorable for navigation. Warren was thought to be the head of navigation on the Allegheny River and was often visited by steamboats from Pittsburgh, during periods of high water.

For the crew making their way home to Russell, Pennsylvania, from Cincinnati, Ohio, the first leg of the journey to Pittsburgh, Pennsylvania, was made by boat, for the sum of $1.50, deck passage. This fare procured a bunk on the main deck, but the men had to furnish or buy their food or bedding during the three-day trip. From Pittsburgh to Warren or Russell, the journey was usually made afoot, as described above. Naturally, the hands were not inclined to spend any more money than necessary in view of the modest amount in their pockets, resulting from their trip downriver on the raft.

Accidents were few and far between, owing to the size and buoyancy of the raft. A raft might strike a bridge pier and break in two, but no one was apt to get hurt in this event. When the raft was to be landed a man would be sent ashore in a skiff, taking with him a cable, the other end of which was tied to the raft. His duty was to select a nearby tree and wind the rope around it before the slack was taken up by the moving raft. Once in a while he might be caught without enough rope by the time he had reached the tree, and would be forced to let go before he had wound the rope around the tree a sufficient number of times to make it fast, in which event it was up to him to throw himself flat on the ground before the end of the cable, whipping around the tree, could hit him with tremendous force. This same accident would sometimes befall a hand in the act of snubbing a cable aboard the raft.

Owing to the crookedness and narrowness of the Conewango Creek and Allegheny River, rafts were not run at night on these streams, except under the most favorable conditions. On the Ohio, running at night was the usual thing, but an unfavorable state of weather or stage of water would occasionally make tying up at night advisable. Fog was the chief obstacle; steamboats would sometimes get hung up on a raft in a fog and have to back off. A pilot's keen knowledge of the river was invaluable, and would also influence the decision on whether or not to run the river at night.

A typical bill of fare on a raft journey would include the following staples: mess pork (salt pork, including ribs) bought by the barrel; potatoes (often from home); raftsmen's biscuits (thick crackers five inches in diameter); coffee and tea; brown sugar; beans; and eggs galore. Whiskey was available in the early days, but was later eliminated from the rations.

In 1904, when a raft was taken apart in Pittsburgh, the lumber sold for 24 cents a cubic foot for pine and 14 cents per cubic foot for hemlock. A cubic foot was equal to twelve board feet.

McKnight in his *Pioneer History of Northwestern Pennsylvania* makes note that the Cornplanter Indians furnished some of the finest raft pilots on the river:

> Their intimate and intuitive knowledge of the water in all stages made their skills invaluable to the craft, and the vast amount of money invested in the immense fleets of lumber rendered their service a very important duty.

Above, 1873, Hickory Street suspension bridge with rafts at high water. Below, more rafts at Warren.   c. 1890.

A part-time occupation during the 1830s and 1840s was the making of roof shingles which were shaped on a schnitzelbunk. Barges were built, filled with shingles, and shipped to Pittsburgh where they were purchased by home builders. These two decades were the peak of the lumbering business on the Allegheny River.

McKnight reports:

> It is a cheering sight to see the bright, broad raft floating slowly down the picturesque passes of the Allegheny, with its little shanties, and busy population; some lifting the long heavy oars, some cooking at the great fire, some eating their bacon from a broad clean shingle—superior to French porcelain—some lounging in the sun, and some practicing their coarse wit upon the gazers from the shore, and making the wild hills echo with their shouts.

This colorful era came to a close early in the twentieth century when Pittsburgh began to receive lumber from Tennessee and Kentucky. Local shipments from the forests of the upper Allegheny River began to go north to Buffalo by railroad. The iron horse had replaced the raft and a grand era had ended.

An appreciation of the heritage of our wild rivers—as a means for exploration, settlement, trade, and commerce—is critical to understanding the growth of a nation. Building a dam on a wild river not only changes the way of life of the people living on the waterway, but it changes the potential uses of that river for centuries. Just as technological changes, such as the introduction of the railroad, forever altered lumbering on the Allegheny River, Kinzua Dam tamed the wild waters of the Allegheny River. Flooding on the Allegheny is abated, the waters are docile—and the tough-minded, rough and ready crews, riding the flood waters with their annual bounty of lumber, are forever gone.

EXPLORERS AND SETTLERS

Experience is not what happens to you; it's what you do with what happens to you.

- Aldous Huxley

In Zeisberger's *Allegheny River Indian Towns: 1767-1770*, it is reported that French maps made before 1700 show that the Allegheny River was part of an almost-all water highway from the East to the West and South. Zeisberger was a Moravian missionary who had been stationed at numerous Indian towns along the upper Allegheny River.

According to Zeisberger this water route enabled explorers to take the Niagara portage from Lake Ontario into Lake Erie and land at what is now known as Barcelona, New York. From Barcelona the travel would be by land, crossing a short *hogsback* path—across the mountain ridges—to again enter water at Chautauqua Lake. Indians and white explorers would travel from Chautauqua Lake into the Conewango Creek and into the Allegheny River at Warren, Pennsylvania.

If the pioneers traveled further west along the shore of Lake Erie than Barcelona, New York, there was a longer land path to Waterford, Pennsylvania, on the head of French Creek. River travel down French Creek meets the Allegheny River at Franklin, Pennsylvania, by-passing Warren.

If Lake Erie and Lake Ontario were to be avoided, then a traveler would transfer from the western head of the Susquehanna River or from the head of the Genesee River to the Allegheny River. All three of these rivers have their sources near one another.

These three water routes were scenes of great activity: exploration, conquest, and commerce. One route in particular, the Chautauqua-Conewango-Allegheny route, was the most heavily traveled, and was to become critical to the exploration of the Allegheny River from Warren and downriver. This particular route was also used as a long line of communication between the old French colonies in Canada and the new colony in Louisiana.

Originally the Allegheny River and the Ohio River were thought of as one river. The Iroquois thought so, and the Seneca name for the river system was O-bee-yah. *Belle Riviere* was the early French name—beautiful river.

The French visited the headwaters of the Allegheny River as early as 1749. Today, a plaque in Celoron Park, Warren, Pennsylvania, notes this early exploration, which claimed this very land for France. The plaque reads:

Pierre Joseph Celoron
Sieur De Blainville

This tablet erected by the
Kanoagoa Chapter National Society
Daughters of the American Colonists
Commemorates the

Seneca Indian Village
Once on the Site of Warren
As stated in the Diaries of
Celoron and Father Bonnechamps
Who buried the Lead Plates near here
At the juncture of the
Conewango Creek and Allegheny River
July 29, 1749

The lead plates, buried at the juncture of the Conewango Creek and the Allegheny River in 1749, have never been located.

Historically important, both militarily and commercially, was the fact that little or nothing of the Allegheny River above Warren, Pennsylvania, was known. Early explorers entered the Allegheny River from the Conewango Creek, and proceeded south to what is now Oil City, Franklin, Pittsburgh, and points beyond—few, if any, ventured north.

John Montour, Brodhead's guide to Warren in 1779, knew nothing of the Allegheny River above the town of Warren. When George Washington was considering a military advance against Fort Niagara by way of the Allegheny River, his guides had to resort to the Indians for information. This advance against Fort Niagara via the Allegheny River was cancelled for lack of information.

Detailed information, regarding these particular waterways, and the people who lived along them, proved to be an essential component, a pivotal point, for the success or failure of military ventures. Due to the white man's lack of knowledgeable guides, the Seneca Indians had been able to maintain a semi-quarantine against explorers and the military, on the land they lived upon and controlled in the upper Allegheny valleys. In the latter half of the eighteenth century this isolation became more difficult to preserve, as settlers found their way into these valleys, rich with furs and virgin timber.

One of the earliest settlers of the upper Allegheny River valley was Philip Tome. Tome wrote a book about his experiences in the wilderness, *Pioneer Life: or Thirty Years a Hunter.* This slim volume is filled with fantastic tall tales and breathtaking escapades of his life in the rough and wild lands of the Allegheny Mountains—when hills and valleys were filled with bears, wildcats, elk, and wolves.

Tome first resided in the Kinzua Valley, in the area of Kinzua Run, about 1816, and served as a hunter, a guide, and occasionally an interpreter for Cornplanter in his dealings with the whites. Philip Tome later left the area and did not return to this part of the state until 1827, when he came to the territory which was to become known as Corydon.

The surname, Tome, and Corydon grew to be nearly synonymous in the recorded history of this valley, upriver from the settlement of Kinzua. Ruth Tome Funk, the great-granddaughter of Philip Tome, recalled much about Corydon, and with the help of her niece, Ruth Prue Burgett, many facts were preserved in *Corydon-In Remembrance*. Ruth's genealogy was: Jacob Tome; Philip Tome; Benjamin Tome; George Lundy Tome; and Ruth Tome Funk.

The last teacher at the Cornplanter School across the Allegheny River was Lucia Wilcox Browne, cousin of Ruth, and also a great-granddaughter of Philip Tome. Corydon and the Cornplanter Grant maintained a close and cooperative relationship. After attending school on the Cornplanter Grant, the Cornplanters had the option of going to high school in Corydon or Kinzua.

The Corydon School, a large, two-story wooden building, had four grades to a room on the first floor, with the high school located on the second floor. By the late 1930s, the high school was closed, and students attended high school in Bradford, Pennsylvania. During earlier times there were other schools in the Corydon area: Willow Creek had two one-room schools and the Byron Tome School was located farther up Willow Creek.

When a post office, set up for the Cornplanters across the river from the Grant at Gowango, was closed, mail and provisions were picked up by the Cornplanters at the Corydon Post Office. The Cornplanter Indians were the closest neighbors to the settlers of Corydon. All peacefully co-existed and prospered in this rustic, hidden valley of the Allegheny Mountains. Corydon Township, originally part of McKean County, became part of Warren County on March 20, 1846.

Lumbering was the economic base of the community. According to *Corydon-In Remembrance*, the Albany Company commenced their lumber business in Corydon in 1852. Plank roads were built at this time to ease the transport of lumber to the river, where it would commence its journey to Pittsburgh. In 1867, the Allegheny Valley Railroad was built and Corydon entered into its boom years, becoming a solid and prosperous lumbering and farming community. By the 1880s, the Buffalo, New York, and Philadelphia Railroad had come to town. Corydon now had two hotels and eleven businesses, not counting the grist mill, the livery stable, a tool handle factory, and several busy blacksmiths.

Corydon was also very popular with hunters and fishermen—nature's abundance was everywhere. A hotel, the Corydon House, was built in the mid-1800s to accommodate these sportsmen. Additions were later made to the hotel, including a third story ballroom. At one time there was an old dirt and log dam on the Allegheny River across from the Corydon House. This was a very popular fishing spot and attracted many out-of-towners to Corydon. The Corydon House was sold in May of 1925. It never again operated as a hotel and was eventually purchased by the federal government, as was all the Corydon property.

Another hotel, the Maple Shade Hotel, was built by the Boyer family in Corydon. Legend has it that Philip Tome wrote *Pioneer Life: or Thirty Years a Hunter* at the Maple Shade.

The river always dominated and influenced the lives of all who lived along it, and depended on it for transportation and food. Ingenious ways were developed to make the most of all available resources. Early settlers used johnboats when the river was manageable. These boats were long and narrow and the user stood in the middle of the boat and pushed with a pole. *Corydon—In Remembrance* records that jackboats were used for night fishing. These were similar to johnboats, but were rigged with large pieces of tin or zinc placed on the boat ends where knots of *Jack Pine* were fastened and burned. When night fishing, three people were often required for the expedition to be a success: one person to pole the boat; one person to keep the pine knot fire going; and one person to spear the fish. There were many fish in the river and no fishing laws—large catches were divided up among members of the community.

By the 1890s Corydon could boast of two ferries operating in its vicinity. The lower ferry on the Allegheny River was used by the Cornplanter Indians when coming to Corydon. The ferry on the upper Allegheny River, now in the Webb Ferry area, was used by the Quaker Hill and State Line neighbors when visiting or doing business in Corydon. These ferries were not only used for transporting people, but also for farm products, lumber, saw mill machinery, and livestock.

All were not consumed with only work though, as in the 1900s baseball was a favorite activity in the valley and the topic of many conversations. Corydon, Kinzua, and Onoville supported baseball teams, as did the Seneca Reservation. Ruth Tome Funk records that Corydon's own Ray Caldwell graduated to the major leagues from his modest beginning with the Corydon ox-roast ball games. Ray was reported to have had a fast ball with a formidable whiplash curve. His major league career started with the New York Yankees and finished with the Cleveland Indians. He pitched to some of the greats, such as Walter Johnson, Ty Cobb, Tris Speaker, and the likes of the great George Herman Ruth (Babe Ruth).

Telephone service had reached Corydon by the early 1900s. It was a private enterprise started by Asa Reeves of Corydon, and was later purchased by Dr. Clayton Flatt. Small switchboards were placed in Corydon and Kinzua with the phone line run up the Allegheny Valley to the settlements of Willow Creek-Stickney area, Sugar Run, and other outlying areas. The telephone lines in these very rural areas were faithfully maintained for many years by Roy Bennett, a Cornplanter Indian.

The Corydon Methodist Episcopal Church had its groundbreaking ceremony on August 30, 1883. The last service was held on August 5, 1962, as the church was sold to the U.S. Army Corps of Engineers as part of the Kinzua Dam project.

A prayer of dispersal, the singing of hymns, and the final benediction closed the church. The furnishings were distributed among other Methodist Episcopal churches.

Rarely did settlers willingly leave the valley, and farms were often never out of the family. Philip Tome's land was handed down to Benjamin Tome, then to George Lundy Tome in 1867. George Lundy Tome was born, November 2, 1845, and died in 1939. For part of his life he was a river pilot. He also collaborated with Professor William Armstrong of New Jersey on a book, *Hunting the Wild Pigeon.*

The Tome land then went to Cynthia Tome Prue in 1915, and so on, until the land was purchased by the federal government for construction of Kinzua Dam. Homes and businesses were vacated by individuals and families, who accepted government settlements from the U.S. Army Corps of Engineers; but 23 families, who steadfastly wished to remain in their Corydon homes, were eventually evicted by U.S. Marshals.

Philip Tome, the first white settler of Corydon, died in 1855. He was buried with his wife in a cemetery in Corydon, on land which he donated to the village. Harry Tome, Philip Tome's great-great-grandson, was the last resident to leave Corydon. Eight months after the post office closed—and finally, when all electricity to the village had been turned off—Harry Tome departed, but not easily, and definitely not by choice. The town was razed in preparation for flooding by the Allegheny Reservoir.

The graves from the Corydon Cemetery were moved above flood waters to the Riverview Cemetery near Willow Bay. This cemetery was expanded to include the Corydon re-interment, just as it was expanded to receive the graves from the Cornplanter Grant. The Riverview Cemetery today is really three separate cemeteries. Enter the single gate of the cemetery and the Cornplanter burials are to the right, the Corydon burials to the left, and the original Riverview site is to the back, nearest the Allegheny Reservoir.

The Riverview Cemetery is located on a gentle slope overlooking the reservoir. The surrounding hills are heavily forested, and Cornplanter's grave and monument command the hilltop. Many pioneers, settlers, and Indians now lay claim to this hillside, but willingly share the view with visitors wanting to pay tribute to the talent and courage of these rugged individuals.

A great deal of legend is entwined in the history that chronicles the lives of those who roamed, hunted, and settled in these deep valleys. One legend told is that Aaron Burr stopped in Kinzua about 1805, shortly after he killed Alexander Hamilton.

Burr was on his way westward, where he intended to create an empire. He needed help and supplies, and as legend goes, encouraged settlers, including the Morrisons of Kinzua Valley, to join him in his travels. Burr camped on Morrison Island, near where the Kinzua Creek entered the Allegheny River. The Kinzua settlers resisted his offer of travel, fed him, and sent him on his way.

James Morrison was one of many Revolutionary War soldiers who played an important role in settling this area. He first came to Warren County in 1799 and originally made his home on an island near Kinzua in 1801, the same island, according to legend, on which Aaron Burr camped. Morrison's descendants were leaders in the milling business and the settling of the Kinzua Valley. James Morrison died in 1830.

One of the biggest landowners in the Kinzua area, Indians aside, was Smith Labree. Labree arrived in 1815 and came to own most of the land that made up the village of Kinzua. He made his living in lumber and as a river pilot. On his arrival at Kinzua Creek, Labree found only three clearings in the forest. There were two small clearings and a large one made by the Indians, as this was a popular fishing spot for the Senecas. As there were no roads, travel was by water or foot. Labree, born in 1797, lived until 1860; and in that time he saw the Kinzua area become settled and prosperous.

There are many other names in the early history of Kinzua and Corydon. Enoch Gillam built the first mill in Corydon. Simeon Marsh, a Revolutionary War soldier from New Jersey, also settled in the valley. There were many more who built the valley into a bustling lumber center, where rafts were made up for the long trip downstream. Friendly Seneca Indians made this all the more achievable. The peaceful existence of white settlers, near Indians who treasured their land and way of life, was due in part to the influence of Cornplanter. These valleys with their winding, still untamed river, and thickly timbered slopes were the home for more than a century and a half to the descendants of sturdy pioneers, who carved for themselves productive farms and prosperous settlements.

Early 20th century views of Corydon, Pennsylvania.

Kinzua Post Office and
Saint Luke's Church, above.
Old Route 59 road sign for
the village of Kinzua, right.
A scene of summer at its
peak, along the banks of
Kinzua Creek, below. c.1958.

Schools are central in maintaining the ongoing spirit of every community, and the Kinzua Township School served its community for 80 years. It was built in 1882 and closed at the end of the 1961-62 school year.

History records that in 1881 an acre of ground was purchased on Blackman Street in the village of Kinzua to build a new school. Bids ranged from $3,800 to $5,000. All bids were rejected because they were too high. The school board decided it could do better.

John MacLean of Sugar Grove, Pennsylvania, was employed for $18.00 to draft specifications for the new school building and to buy materials that the school board did not already have on hand. Mr. MacLean also served as head carpenter for $2.75 per day and board. Other carpenters earned $2.00 per day. Ed Strong received $3.00 per day for his work as head stone cutter. The final cost of the building was $5,000. As luck would have it, the cost was identical to the high bid originally received by the school board.

On October 16, 1882, the Board of Control decided to start using the new school. The first teachers were O. J. Gunning, principal, and Lizzie Jackson and Dora Allen. Besides being principal and teacher, Mr. Gunning's daily duties also included building the fire and keeping the rooms and halls cleaned. For this he received an annual salary of $600.00.

The first high school class graduated in 1895. In September of 1911, a three-year high school was instituted which continued until 1926, when a four-year high school was organized. This high school continued until 1942, when the students were moved to Warren, Pennsylvania. On January 14, 1953, Kinzua entered the Warren Area Joint School District and all grades were moved to Warren, with the exception of the first six which remained at Kinzua. Two rooms were used at the Kinzua School, and the final teachers were Mrs. Louise Mann and Mrs. Margaret Coates. Each teacher taught three grades.

During the last two years the school was open, it had to accommodate the children of construction workers for Kinzua Dam. This placed a large financial burden on the township. Since the construction workers lived on what was government-owned land, they did not pay local taxes which would have supported Kinzua School. The cost per pupil per month was about $32.00 for the township. The workers resided nearby, but not, in fact, among the local citizens. It's ironic that while the men worked and dwelled in this beautiful valley, the results of their labor assured that no one would ever live in these fated hamlets yet again. They worked hard for good pay. It was not their intention to displace people from their homes in *discontinued* towns, as the government would phrase it, but the end result was the same. Undoubtedly, there were lawyers, and timber merchants, among others, who traded upon misfortune during these ungentle times. Towns, farms, stores, homes, and schools were dismembered and deleted.

The Kinzua School closed upon termination of the 1961-62 school year, as did the Corydon School. The Corydon School building and the land were sold to the United States government through the U.S. Army Corps of Engineering Real Estate Division for $6,500. At that time the government also purchased the Kinzua Township School and land for $19,700.

Kinzua High School and the "Triangle" business area, Kinzua.

Saint Luke's Episcopal Church in the village of Kinzua was a charming, pictur-
esque stone building often featured on postcards from the area. Travelers to this
pastoral valley would frequently have their pictures taken in front of the church.

A small wood-framed chapel was the first Episcopal Church in this close-knit
community. The cornerstone for the frame structure was laid at an outdoor service on Saint Luke's Day in 1889. The chapel was consecrated on September 20,
1892. Only eight years later, it was destroyed by fire on February 6, 1900. The
new building, *the little stone church*, was completed in 1901, and the date of con-
secration was 1904.

The new church was built of native stone, chipped and hewn on the site. For
a sense of continuity, the old cornerstone from the first church was placed in the
new building at the northwest corner. The last Kinzua service at Saint Luke's
Episcopal Church was on March 18, 1962. The church was deconsecrated on this
date.

Saint Luke's Episcopal Church, Kinzua, Pennsylvania, 1961.

By the spring of 1962 the town of Kinzua was in the painful process of a slow death—as well as the Allegheny communities of Corydon and Morrison. The 1960 census reported Kinzua Township, officially organized in 1821, had a population of 468 residents, the largest portion of which resided in the village of Kinzua.

All the property within the 32 mile-long high water area of the Allegheny River reservoir, under the 1,365-foot flood control pool elevation, was to be eventually acquired by the government. The original estimate by the U.S. Corps of Engineers for the town of Kinzua was that 1,100 to 1,600 tracts of property had to be handled—appraised, purchased, condemned—and ultimately acquired by the government.

In preparation for flooding, the land was cleared. The reservoir basin was cleared to the 1,328-foot level, the summer pool. From that point to the 1,365 level, the maximum pool, the basin was also cleared of brush and any floatable materials. This area was deemed *usable* by the Army Corps of Engineers when water levels were low, but not *livable,* as it would occasionally be flooded during periods of high water. The Army Corps set its *taking area* to 300 feet beyond the 1,365 level. By March 15 of 1962 ninety percent of the village of Kinzua was in United States government ownership.

Kinzua Valley, the school may be seen to the left. c.1960.
Below, the same valley cleared, burned, and ready for
inundation by the waters of the Allegheny Reservoir. 1966.

In early October, 1966, the last public business and private home were put to the torch by the Army Corps of Engineers in what was once the village of Onoville, New York. This was nearly the end of what was the systematic razing of every structure in the entire Kinzua Valley before the Allegheny Reservoir engulfed the homes, farms, and villages where generations of descendants of the earliest settlers, who came in the late 1700s, were born and reared.

The last two Onoville, New York, structures to be razed were the Red Wing Tavern and the nearby residence of Mr. and Mrs. Carl Burch. A local tradition claimed that the century-old Red Wing Tavern had once been a stage coach inn. The tavern was rebuilt near the new highway, above the waterline of the Allegheny Reservoir.

Carl Burch had built his home thirty years earlier in Onoville. He was a master carpenter who had carried his tool box across the continent four times, and back to his home in Onoville. One particularly important construction job he worked on was near Las Vegas, Nevada, for the Atomic Energy Commission. It was directly related to the first testing of the atomic bomb.

Burch helped build two typical houses at the Nevada site. One of the houses was a quarter-mile and the other was a half-mile from the point the atomic bomb was first tested by detonation in Nevada. Both houses were completely wired, furnished, and fully functioning in every sense. Inside the houses were life-sized dummies of men and women. The purpose was to learn the effect of a nuclear blast on buildings, furnishings, and people. Reports of the tests were widely publicized at the time, in newspapers, magazines, television, and movies.

Burch reportedly mused as he watched his Onoville home burn, saying: "All I have left is my case of carpenter tools, and it's kinda rusty." A boat launching facility for the new reservoir was built on the site of his home.

The Burch home was vacated at 10:00 a.m., October 2, 1966. It was set afire by the U.S. Army Corps of Engineers at 10:30 a.m. The home was reduced to ashes within the hour. This action nearly completed the systematic razing of every structure in the entire Kinzua Valley.

All that remained of the New York community of Onoville was a former schoolhouse, whose final use was as an engineer's temporary office, before it, too, was razed.

To build the dam the U.S. Corps of Engineers had acquired 1,280 properties and relocated or replaced 495 houses, 385 hunting or vacation cabins, 50 businesses, 9 churches, and 2 schools.

After the Allegheny Reservoir had filled, there were recurring periods of low water. The waters of the Allegheny Reservoir reached an all-time low on

November 24, 1991. The reservoir had shrunk to half its normal water size—after a winter of lower than normal snowfall, and a summer of drought.

Remnants of former human occupation, thought by all to be forever beneath the waters of the reservoir, were revealed for the first time since the gates on Kinzua Dam were closed. The receding water revealed many of the fractured remains of Corydon: the stone fence around the cemetery; cement steps of the school; foundations of houses. A small number of gravestones were also revealed. This surprised and alarmed the surviving family members of the early settlers, as it was promised by the U.S. Army Corps of Engineers that all burial plots and headstones were to have been safely re-interred. At this time, the Corps of Engineers responded by saying that most of the headstones and plots had been relocated, but some of the headstones could not be removed due to their poor condition.

Odd as it seems, if a curious visitor removed any artifact over 50 years old from the exposed reservoir floor, he would be committing a federal offense—removal of artifacts being strictly prohibited and subject to fine. Visitors were restricted to simply viewing firsthand the remains of the town. If deemed so important by law, and if reportedly subject to removal by curious individuals; why were not all headstones initially removed by the Corps of Engineers? Two of the mystery headstones revealed Corydon names of *Knapp* and *Marriah*. One hundred eighty-nine Corydon gravesites were purportedly moved to the expanded Riverview Cemetery during Kinzua Dam construction. The original Corydon Cemetery had a recorded history from 1819 to 1963.

Cemetery relocation was not only for Cornplanter Indian gravesites, Allegany Reservation Indian remains, and Corydon, but also for remains in Kinzua and Morrison Run cemeteries. In the 1962 relocation of Kinzua and Morrison Run cemeteries, 1,361 graves, including bodies, monuments, and markers, were re-interred in the Willow Dale Cemetery in West Branch, located about three miles west of Bradford, Pennsylvania, on Route 346. The U.S. Corps of Engineers awarded the Kinzua-Morrison gravesite relocation contract to low bidder, E.L. Colburn Company of Westville, Oklahoma, for $187,887. The law required that every grave in every cemetery affected by Kinzua Dam and the Allegheny Reservoir be moved to a new and approved site.

After the Allegheny Reservoir had filled, there were recurring periods of low water. The waters of the Allegheny Reservoir reached an all-time low on November 24, 1991. The Reservoir had shrunk to half its normal water size—after a winter of lower than normal snowfall and a summer of drought. These images are from Corydon, 1998, when low water again occurred.

Camp Olmstead, property of the Chief Cornplanter Council, Boy Scouts of America, being located adjacent to the Cornplanter Grant, was affected by the construction of Kinzua Dam. Camp Olmstead, bordering the Allegheny River, was located immediately south of the Cornplanter Grant. Approximately one-third of the acreage of Camp Olmstead property was covered by the waters of the reservoir.

Having been purchased in 1927 by George Olmstead from Alice V. Tuttle, administrator of the Nathan Tuttle estate, the Boy Scout Council was in posses-sion of approximately 270 acres on the west bank of the Allegheny River. The land was transferred to what was then known as the Boy Scout Council for Warren County. In 1954, it became the Chief Cornplanter Council. The two-thirds of the remaining acreage of the camp, above the high water mark of the reservoir, were sufficient for the council's continued operation. Camp Olmstead remains active today.

WATER—WATER—IT'S THE CRY EVERYWHERE

In rivers and bad governments, the lightest things swim at the top.

~ Benjamin Franklin (1706–1790)

Hell hath no fury like a bureaucrat scorned.

~ Milton Friedman

In June, 1945, a canalization project of the upper Allegheny River was formally put forward by Representative L. H. Gavin of Oil City. Representative Gavin took the lead in Congress in seeking a study by the U.S. Army Corps of Engineers of the feasibility of improving the Allegheny River for navigation. Opponents to the Kinzua Dam took courage from this move on the part of Gavin, for if the Allegheny River were to be developed for slack water navigation then the dam could not be built.

On June 23, 1947, the Fiftieth Anniversary Convention of the Allegheny River Improvement Association pledged its full support for the creation, maintenance, and use of inland waterways. Among the officers elected at the Fiftieth Anniversary was Harold Chase Putnam of Warren, Pennsylvania. The Association opposed the construction of any *super-dams,* such as Kinzua, which would prevent the integration of the nation's inland waterways. They believed that cheap water transportation to and from the east coast was the key to industrial survival in western Pennsylvania and New York State.

There was a plea from the Association for improvements of the Allegheny River for barge navigation. With these improvements it was predicted that there would be large tows of barges moving up and down an improved Allegheny River. A connection with the reconstructed Genesee Valley Canal would permit the carrying of coal, oil, and finished manufactured goods and imports from New York harbor into the mid-continent by way of the Allegheny and Ohio rivers.

The Sunday, November 16, 1947, issue of the *Erie Dispatch* ran a piece on *The Allegheny—Pride of Warren*, where it was claimed that the Allegheny River was perhaps the largest unimproved river east of the Rocky Mountains. Asserting the Allegheny as one of America's great rivers and knowing that any great river can be all things in all of its moods—"cruel enough to take a life, hospitable enough to feed and clothe," if indirectly, an entire area; the Upper Allegheny River Improvement Association, headquartered in Warren, continued its efforts to see the upper Allegheny improved with navigational facilities similar to those near Pittsburgh, Pennsylvania.

The Association's goal was to have the entire river linked with the New York State great system of canals and rivers. This was the proposed ocean-to-gulf waterway. One pamphlet of the Upper Allegheny River Improvement Association said the following in regard to the Allegheny.

> Our mighty Allegheny is strategically located to complete a vast navigable inland waterway from New York harbor to New Orleans. The advantages are so tremendous that the engineering problems shrink into insignificance by comparison. The

know-how, money, materials, and manpower are available. All
that is lacking is the will.

The Association worked diligently to provide the will to accomplish these
goals. It pointed out that by building the *Allegheny Riverway* the entire region
would profit by having great commercial and recreational advantages—industries
would multiply in the river valley due to the cheap means of transportation for
materials and goods.

At this time, 1947, navigational improvements on the Allegheny River
stopped at the town of East Brady, Pennsylvania—about 72 miles above the
river's mouth at Pittsburgh. Business, industry, and branches of the government
plotted ways and means to get their desired profit out of the Allegheny River. As
always, the mighty Allegheny River rolled on, waiting for no man or government.

In 1953, the U.S. Army Corps of Engineers literally blasted canalization. The
Corps reported that slack water navigation from Pittsburgh to Rochester—via the
Allegheny River and a rejuvenated Genesee Valley canal from Olean, to connect
with the state barge canal—would be physically possible, but would cost nearly a
billion dollars! Annual maintenance costs were projected to be fifty million dollars. The Corps of Engineers decided that returns in the way of revenues and economic advantages would not be commensurate to the initial investment and cost
of maintenance. The engineers advised the House Public Works Committee that
canalization would be impractical. This report was devastating for those in favor
of canalizing the Allegheny River by a system of locks, but a boost for those in
favor of building the Kinzua Dam.

The billion dollars projected for canalization made the costs of Kinzua Dam
appear miniscule in comparison. Cost of the dam project in 1940 was estimated
at $30,000,000; cost in 1953 was estimated at $66,000,000. Final costs in 1966
were $116,000,000 for completion of Kinzua Dam and the Allegheny
Reservoir—one-tenth the projected costs of canalization, according to the Corps
of Engineers.

In 1957, a Kinzua Dam protest meeting attracted overflow crowds from Kinzua,
Corydon, and elsewhere along the Allegheny Valley. It was held in the packed
Kinzua Fire Hall and overflowed into the streets. Speaking was Edward O'Neil,
attorney for the Seneca Nation of Indians. O'Neil stated that the current impetus
given the Kinzua Dam project was a result of direct Congressional pressure
brought about by Pittsburgh industries in trouble for Allegheny River pollution.
In addition to being a massive flood protection project, those protesting against
dam construction soon realized the dam was also to be a water pollution project—designed to keep industry from violating government dictated pollution

standards along the Allegheny River—particularly when the river reached its low and dangerously acidic stage in late summer.

Pollution abatement for the industrial cities of the lower Allegheny River, primarily Pittsburgh, Pennsylvania, was of growing importance. Elimination of diseases, originating in rivers fouled by our growing industrial society, of which, Pittsburgh was a prime contributor at this time, had always been an objective of the Corps of Engineers, as so directed by the U.S. Congress. All along the Allegheny River there was a growing need for the combination of an adequate, controlled water supply and the construction of water treatment plants. These were to result in a bacteria count for the river sufficiently low to assure healthy conditions.

Not only were floods to be avoided, but so were the parched streambeds of summer, when the river would be most susceptible to pollution. Water from the relatively pure, upper Allegheny River would be stored during the spring flood period, and released gradually in the summer, helping to purify the Allegheny River during the low water season. The proposed Allegheny Reservoir would control a 2,180-square-mile watershed, the largest uncontrolled watershed that remained in western Pennsylvania.

Richard Morrison of Kinzua, descendant of one of the valley's earliest settlers, moderated the first organized protest meeting in Kinzua. Residents of Kinzua and other small communities joined together to form the *Save Our Valley Committee*, with Morrison as President.

Prior to the 1957 formation of this protest committee, the residents of the valley had been lulled into a false sense of security, mostly by what appeared as long periods of inactivity on the part of the federal government in regard to construction of Kinzua Dam. Things were about to change.

Congressman L. H. Gavin of the 23rd District, before the Public Works Subcommittee, House Appropriations Committee, regarding the Allegheny River Reservoir project, May 15, 1957, stated most succinctly: "Water. Water. It is the cry everywhere."

In 1958, the Ohio Valley Improvement Association (OVIA), a group of industrial and government interests, submitted a report to the federal House and Senate appropriations subcommittee. OVIA asked for increased spending on flood control and navigation improvements in the Ohio River basin, including a $5,000,000 boost in Kinzua Dam funds.

OVIA's total request for the coming year was for expenditures of $110,000,000. Their reasoning for the necessity of such vast sums differed from much of the other discussions of the time—that is, the need for flood control and pollution abatement in the Ohio River basin. OVIA's requests were designed to cope with the recession. An economic slump had hit basic industries—steel, coal, aluminum, and chemical—of the Ohio Valley basin. Unemployment in the Ohio Valley was at a much higher level than the nation as a whole.

An even greater divergence from the flood control and pollution abatement reasoning was Hudson Biery's, OVIA's executive vice president at the time, national defense approach. Biery stated:

> A clean water reserve...would be priceless in the event of a nuclear attack that would contaminate the usual sources of supply. It is no foolish fear...the sooner we get our reservoirs finished and our greater capacity high level navigation dams on the Ohio River, the greater will be our ability to snap back from the terrors of such a catastrophe, should it ever come.

Being the height of the Cold War era, it is not surprising that national defense was an approach used in requests for increased expenditures for public works. Extremely alarming was the notion that we could *snap back* from a nuclear attack, let alone that we could maintain this massive system as a clean water reserve. Kinzua Dam was to be an important component of this system, and these ramifications were being felt by the communities on the headwaters of the Allegheny River.

Opponents to the dam were at times optimistic, but in hindsight it is certain some spoke prematurely. Edward O'Neil, Seneca Nation attorney leading the Seneca Indian battle to halt construction of the dam, was encouraged by Congressional refusal to allow the Army Corps of Engineers to spend their latest million-dollar appropriation. He declared that time was in favor of the opponents to Kinzua Dam. In June, 1958, O'Neil stated:

> Kinzua Dam is weakening day by day. The protest is growing across the country, and time is now in our favor. I was in a hurry (in the courts) but no longer.

Although plans for Kinzua Dam had been on the books of the Corps of Engineers since the late 1930s, nothing concrete was done by opponents of the dam for twenty years. During the early 1950s, Warren was fractured in its support of the Kinzua Dam and the Allegheny Reservoir. Most were particularly vehement in denouncing the project. No one in Warren, it seemed, was particularly interested in living a short distance below a great dam. Despite flooding, there was a desire by many for no change.

Among some Warren residents there was a small following for the Morgan Plan—a means of diverting flood waters by a series of smaller dams into Lake Erie. There was also limited interest in promoting river navigation and improving the state's canal system for river craft and barges.

A *Pittsburgh Post-Gazette* story ran under the heading of *Warren Victim of Apathy.* This story supported those few people in favor of the Kinzua project. It pointed out that if the massive dam and reservoir on the Allegheny River had been built, as proposed long ago, many citizens would have been spared much property damage and suffering. Colonel Harold E. Sprague, District Engineer of the U.S. Army Corps of Engineers, wrote in the *Greater Pittsburgh Magazine* of October, 1955:

> The Allegheny Reservoir above Warren, Pennsylvania, the largest unit by far in the entire system (of flood control) has not materialized, most probably because of public apathy. At the same time regulation of the discharge during the winter season by the Allegheny Reservoir would be helpful in preventing ice gorges, for which the Allegheny River is notorious. In both winter and summer, the discharge would be sufficient to neutralize the acid condition in the lower Allegheny and provide enough alkalinity to benefit the upper Ohio. This would be of great value to both industrial and domestic users who are now forced to neutralize water drawn from the Allegheny and Ohio.

The following image demonstrates the destructive powers of the Allegheny River in both winter and spring. During the winter of 1918, Corydon suffered devastation from enormous ice dams that forced their way into the village, tearing homes and businesses from their foundations. The devastation to property was immense. Many settlers of Corydon were almost willing to ride their homestead down the river on a huge slab of ice, rather than simply abandon it to the forces of the Allegheny River. In 1956, spring floods are shown inundating residential streets of Warren—the milkman patiently waits for his customers to arrive by canoe.

Destructive ice dams and floods in Corydon, 1918, above.
Spring floods inundating the streets of Warren, 1956, below.

The struggle to save Corydon homes and property from the ravages of the Allegheny River during the harsh winter of 1918 is expressed in a letter from *In Remembrance*. The letter is from Ruth Tome Funk's sister, Cynthia, in Corydon, to their sister, Nell, at Salamanca, New York.

> February 16, 1918
>
> Corydon, Pennsylvania
>
> Dear Nell,
>
> I don't know if you will get this letter or not, but I will try to get it to the railroad. The ice and water are very high and our old home may not be here as the water is now over the second step on the front porch. Your bungalow is over the second step on the front porch. Your bungalow is packed in huge ice cakes and water running over the top. George and Hank have been going through the ice and water to get things out and storing them in the barn. We have lifted everything from the first floor of our own place. They have tied cables around your bungalow to the orchard trees, hoping to hold it. The Fitzpatrick House, the blacksmith shop, Everett's store, and many other buildings are already gone. The water is running through many houses. All poles, trees, and fences from the State Line to Willow Creek are down or gone. Looking from our house across the river, water is everywhere, just one big lake.
>
> Love,
>
> Cynth

Nell's bungalow was lost despite all efforts to save it. Also lost were McClintock's Undertaking Parlor, the hardware store, the barber shop, Woodbeck's Blacksmith shop, the Corydon Post Office, and the McClintock, Kennedy, Turney and Fitzpatrick houses, among others.

Pennsylvania's governor, Brambaugh, sent in the National Guard from Warren and Bradford to help and to assist with the clean up efforts. The governor also sent in demolition experts to dynamite the ice dams and to get the roads open. Amazingly, there was no loss of life due to the 1918 ice dams and floods in Corydon, but the village had a hard time regaining its vigor. Some businesses were not replaced.

Floods have a long history on the Allegheny River. In 1865 the great floods of the upper Allegheny Valley completely demolished Indian villages. Many log cabins were lifted from insecure foundations and crushed along islands and on the river's banks. History records that the March floods of 1865, in Warren, saw the Allegheny River rise to 17.4 feet; 16.8 feet in 1873; and in March of 1913, 15.5 feet. At mid-morning on March 8, 1956, the Allegheny River passed the previous record of 17.4 feet.

In 1956, Warren was isolated by these record flood waters. Times Square, a downtown restaurant, was under three feet of water. On March 8, the south side and west end streets of Warren were turned into veritable rivers. Hundreds of families were evacuated while fire departments launched rescue operations and Civil Defense personnel set up centers for handling emergency situations. The State Armory was established as a refuge center for evacuees. Flood waters curtailed operations at Warren General Hospital and the west wing had to be evacuated. Critically ill patients were moved to the third floor, while others were relocated to emergency beds quickly setup at Warren State Hospital.

1898 flood, Warren, above.
1948 flood, Pa. Ave. and Market St., Warren, below.

After the record high waters of the 1956 floods receded, support of the dam and reservoir significantly increased among civic leaders in Warren. By a vote of 15 to 1, the Warren Borough Council, at the March, 1956, meeting went on record as approving the construction of the Kinzua Dam. The 1956 flood in Warren had inundated hundreds of homes and caused the evacuation of nearly 3,000 people. Even after these devastating floods, popular opinion on the dam continued to vary widely, and heated discussions were often the rule in public meetings.

Once the elected representatives of Warren came to an agreement in support of the dam, they decided to take their consensus to Washington, D.C. Warren's demand was that action be speeded up on the construction of the dam. The delegation from Warren met with the Public Works Subcommittee of the House and Senate Appropriations Committee. In Washington the delegation was joined by Governor David L. Lawrence and Dr. Maurice K. Goddard, Secretary of Forests and Waters.

The makeup of the Warren delegation to Washington, D.C., represented most local industries and civic organizations. The group wanted to provide an emphatic answer to the opponents of the dam, who argued that the community of Warren was against construction. For the first time, in appearance at least, the Warren area was united in favor of construction of Kinzua Dam and the Allegheny Reservoir. Pressure was now applied relentlessly by civic leaders and elected representatives of Warren County for completion of an integrated dam and reservoir in the headwaters of the Allegheny River.

This delegation, on their excursion to the nation's capitol, experienced a major fright—the Associated Press headline for the Warren paper of Thursday, April 30, 1959, reported in large bold type: "AREA DELEGATION ON CHARTERED AIRLINER HAS SCARE." The story continued:

> An anonymous phone call placed in Warren at 8:37 this morning to Allegheny Airlines in Bradford launched a full scale federal investigation, when the caller advised airline officials that the chartered plane headed for Washington, D.C., with 25 Warren County executives aboard, was carrying a bomb, due to explode when the plane touched the Capitol airport.

The Federal Bureau of Investigation with Washington police swung into action. A thorough search of the aircraft failed to reveal any bomb or explosive aboard. Mr. Krause, head of Allegheny Airlines in Utica, New York, in 1959, stated that the bomb scare was a federal offense and that the FBI would waste little time in tracking down the person or persons responsible—"even though the incident should prove to be the work of some crackpot opposing the Kinzua Dam project." On May 2, 1959, FBI agents arrested two sisters for the bomb scare. The sisters said they made the call because they were opposed to the flood control project. They plead guilty—each received one year probation, and each sister was to pay one-half of the court costs.

Discussions on Kinzua Dam came to a climax with President Eisenhower's request for a million dollars to bring *plans* for the project to completion. Kinzua Dam was to be the first major expenditure of federal money on the Allegheny River above Warren, Pennsylvania.

After Congress approved the project, and Eisenhower's million dollars for planning, the Senate added $1,400,000 to the million dollars previously allocated for a total of $2,400,000. In 1959, this was part of the $1,206,000,000 Public Works Bill. President Eisenhower vehemently vetoed this bill because he objected to the addition of 67 projects to the bill—costing an additional $50,000,000. These 67 projects, in 32 states, were not included in Eisenhower's original Public Works Bill.

Many flood-minded taxpayers were eager for resolution of the funding dilemma. Volumes of mail were sent to Congress urging passage of the Public Works Bill, which included Kinzua Dam and other flood control projects in Pennsylvania. There was also considerable mail against construction of Kinzua Dam. Most of the opposition mail was sympathetic to the plight of the Indians.

Senator Joseph H. Clark, Democrat of Pennsylvania, stated he would vote to override the President's veto of the appropriations bill. His Republican colleague, Senator Hugh Scott, was indecisive. Congressman L. H. Gavin, of Oil City, who represented Warren and six other counties, was also reportedly indecisive on the veto override. Congressman Gavin was initially against the dam, but when the 1956 flood waters emptied the Warren hospital and threatened many lives in his district, he was forced to listen to the angry mood of flood victims and the growing tide of public reaction in favor of dam construction. Congressman Gavin quickly became a very vocal supporter of the Kinzua Dam project. Nevertheless, the media reported that Gavin was indecisive—irresolute up to the day before the vote on Eisenhower's veto. Interestingly, there is no record in the House of Representatives on how the various congressmen voted on the original bill submitted to Eisenhower, as it was a voice vote.

Efforts were made to bring back congressmen from all points in the country for the impending vote on the President's veto. At the time, Congress had 285 Democrats and 153 Republicans. Congressman Gavin thought that the Democrats would go solidly for an override.

Some Republican congressmen faced a problem. They had pushed for projects in their districts which were part of the bill, but at the same time were in agreement with the President's belief that the public works projects underway at the time should be finished first. Other projects should be tackled, but ongoing projects should be paid for before new costs were undertaken.

Mayor Thomas J. Gallagher of Pittsburgh sent many telegrams to elected representatives urging the override of the President's veto. In telegrams to Pennsylvania's two senators and Allegheny County's four congressmen, Mayor Gallagher, in a bulletin released by the Associated Press, described President Eisenhower's veto as an example of "short-sighted economy."

Confident House Democrats had figured on picking up quite a few Republican ballots. Republican leaders pitched their plea to their members on party loyalty and fiscal responsibility. Some Republicans had urged the President not to veto the bill because it involved projects in many Republican districts. A veto could adversely affect the political future of the GOP incumbents.

On September 2, 1959, Congress sustained by one vote President Eisenhower's veto of the $1,206,000,000 public works appropriation bill. The roll call vote was 274 in favor of passing the bill over the veto and 138 against. It takes a two-thirds vote of congressional members to override a veto and enact a law over a President's objection. A single switch of a vote would have swung the tally the other way.

In Pennsylvania all 16 Democrats voted to override the veto. They were joined by only two state Republicans; Representatives L. H. Gavin and Carroll D. Kearns. The remainder of the Pennsylvania House delegation, 12 Republicans, voted to sustain Eisenhower's veto.

The House action killed the bill. The Senate had no chance to act on the veto. This outcome held up Eisenhower's record of never having had a veto overridden—although there were to be numerous Presidential vetoes overridden during the remainder of his term in office.

The trillion dollar plus appropriation bill would have provided financing for several hundred public works projects in nearly every congressional district in the country. Most were for river, harbor, and flood control projects. For years this bill had been known as a *pork barrel* bill, and had been a congressional favorite because of popularity in home districts.

On Saturday, May 18, 1963, the House of Representatives Subcommittee on Indian Affairs, of the Committee on Interior and Insular Affairs, met at 10:00 a.m. in the Central High School Auditorium, Salamanca, New York. Congressman James A. Haley, Florida, and chairman of the subcommittee presided. Other House of Representative members on this subcommittee were from the states of Oklahoma, New Mexico, North Carolina, Arizona, Idaho, Virginia, California, Hawaii, Pennsylvania, New York, South Dakota, Ohio, Illinois, California, and North Dakota.

Congressman Haley stated that the purpose of the visit was in the interest of the problems of the Seneca Indians. He further stated that people have a great interest in legislation, but some find it impossible to come to Washington, D.C., to testify. Haley thought it only right and proper that people be heard on any matter affecting their well-being; therefore, the meeting occurred in Salamanca, New York.

Mr. Haley had previously introduced a bill in the 80th Congress—House Joint Resolution 703. At the Salamanca meeting, Haley recalled for those in attendance the gist of the resolution.

Resolution 703 directed the Secretary of the Interior and Secretary of the Army to investigate and report on alternatives to the Kinzua Reservoir project. Those alternatives would then be made available to the U.S. Army Corps of Engineers. Resulting reports called particular attention to potential developments in the Conewango Valley for the storage and discharge of flood waters.

Dr. Morgan, an engineer of note, was retained by the Seneca to study alternatives to the Kinzua Reservoir project. As a result, he sought to block Congressional monetary appropriations for Kinzua Dam by contending that it was not the best plan.

Dr. Morgan thought it would be better to divert flood waters of the upper Allegheny River into the Conewango Valley through the Cattaraugus Creek to Lake Erie. Under this plan water also would be released in the Allegheny River below the cutoff to maintain the flow to Pittsburgh and downstream cities. (*See Map 2.*) At this time the Seneca had already lost their case in the U.S. District Court and the U.S. Supreme Court had refused to grant a *writ of certiorari*, holding that the Seneca land was subject to the same public power of eminent domain as that of other Americans.

The office of the Chief of Engineers, Department of the Army, stated that proposals for the diversion of flood waters from the Allegheny River in the Conewango Valley had been the subject of studies over a period of years. As early as 1928, the Corps of Engineers had considered a general plan involving diversion of waters from the Allegheny River into the Conewango Basin and then into Lake Erie, but had found the plan to be of marginal justification. The Corps reported to the Congressional subcommittee that interest in a diversion scheme was revived in 1957, when an engineering consultant employed by the Seneca Nation of Indians testified before the Appropriations Committee of Congress in support of a diversion plan. The Corps of Engineers stated that since that time a number of alternative plans had been studied by a private engineering firm,

Tippetts-Abett-McCarthy-Stratton (TAMS), employed by the Corps of Engineers. Subsequently, all plans had been studied in detail by the Corps of Engineers.

The engineering firm studied five plans from Dr. Arthur E. Morgan and Mr. Barton Jones, which they considered would cover the principal possibilities for storage in the Conewango Basin and for diversion into Lake Erie. The Corps furnished the results of those plans studied to the Appropriations Committee of Congress.

The Corps of Engineers reported that alternative plans were estimated to cost from 25 to 38 percent more than the project as previously authorized. It would require the taking of from 51 to 108 percent more land and require the dislocation of from 150 to 180 percent more of the resident population.

Based on his consideration of the results of the TAMS studies, as well as a further variation proposed by Dr. Morgan, the consultant hired by the Seneca Nation, the Chief of Engineers of the Corps concluded that the authorized Allegheny Reservoir provided the most economical solution to the water resource development problems of the Allegheny River Basin, and the dam should be constructed as authorized by Congress. It was concluded by the Corps that the advisability of alternative plans had been adequately studied.

Six months after the completion of the TAMS report, Dr. Morgan introduced Morgan Plan number six. Dr. Morgan's further variation submitted for additional study proved to be similar to one of the plans already studied by the private engineering firm of TAMS, except that the plan provided modification to facilitate outlet into Lake Erie via Cattaraugus Creek, in lieu of Silver Creek as in previous studies.

The Chief of Engineers reportedly personally studied the plan of Dr. Morgan, but concluded that the proposal did not provide a solution to the water resource development problems of the Allegheny River Basin that compared favorably with the already authorized plan.

Congressman Haley, subcommittee chairman, who had previously introduced House Joint Resolution 703 bill in the 80th Congress, concluded his report by saying that although he had not been successful with this resolution, his interest had continued in spite of the commencement of the construction of the dam and reservoir which Haley still believed was in direct contradiction to the Treaty of 1794.

Mr. Haley's thoughts were that if the project had been handled by the Committee on Interior and Insular Affairs, the committee he thought should have had jurisdiction, the outcome could have been the same or different; but certainly members of the Seneca Nation would have been given full opportunity to discuss the merits of the project and the location of the dam site.

Mr. Haley next introduced House Resolution 1794. Of course, this new bill could not right a wrong, but it was hoped the subcommittee's work would ease the pain and strain to members of the Seneca Nation by authorizing the acquisition of and payment for a flowage easement and right-of-way over land within the Alleghany Reservation required for the Kinzua project. The bill would also assist the Seneca Nation in its relocation, rehabilitation, and economic development.

House Resolution 1794, as entered by Congressman Haley, provided for assistance designed to improve the economic, social, and educational conditions of enrolled members of the Seneca Nation. It included, but was not limited to, the following purposes:

- Agricultural, commercial, and recreational development on the Allegany, Cattaraugus, and Oil Spring reservations.

- Assistance in industrial development on the Seneca reservations, or within fifty miles of any exterior boundary of said reservations, if a preferential right of employment is granted members of the Seneca Nation.

- The construction and maintenance of community buildings and other community facilities.

- An educational fund for scholarship loans and grants, vocational training, and counseling services.

Haley stressed compassion; nevertheless, he concluded his subcommittee meeting in Salamanca by saying that all must face reality. The dam was under construction and well underway, and before many months the gates would be closed and the lands of the Cornplanter Grant and the Allegany Reservation would be flooded.

For benefit of the congressional record, Congressman Haley again recalled the treaty of November, 1794, between the United States and the tribes of Indians called the Six Nations, signed by Timothy Pickering on behalf of the United States, and by some 60 members of the Six Nations.

Haley also made part of the official record a copy of President Washington's letter to Cornplanter, Half Town, and Great Tree, chiefs and counselors of the Seneca Nation of Indians. The letter was written in Philadelphia and dated December 29, 1790. It was in response to a speech previously made by the Seneca leaders in Philadelphia. It brings to the forefront the concern for mutual friendship, justice, land rights, and unease regarding deception or fraud.

Washington realized the Iroquois spirit of discontent and expressed as he saw it—"the fatherly care the United States intends to take of the Indians."

President Washington's letter follows:

To the Cornplanter, Half Town, and Great Tree, Chiefs and Counselors of the Seneca Nation of Indians.

Philadelphia, December 29, 1790

I the President of the United States, by my own mouth, and by a written speech signed with my own hand [and sealed with the Seal of the U.S.] speak to the Seneka Nation, and desire their attention, and that they would keep this speech in remembrance of the friendship of the United States.

I have received your speech with satisfaction, as a proof of your confidence in the justice of the United States, and I have attentively examined the several objects which you have laid before me, whether delivered by your Chiefs at Tioga Point in the last month to Colonel Pickering, or laid before me in the present month by the Cornplanter and the other Seneca Chiefs now in Philadelphia.

In the first place I observe to you, and I request it may sink deep in your minds, that it is my desire, and the desire of the United States that all the miseries of the late war should be forgotten and buried forever. That in future the United States and the Six Nations should be truly brothers, promoting each other's prosperity by acts of mutual friendship and justice.

I am not uninformed that the Six Nations have been led into some difficulties with respect to the sale of their lands since the peace. But I must inform you that these evils arose before the present government of the United States was established, when the separate States and individuals under their authority, undertook to treat with Indian tribes respecting the sale of their lands.

But the case is now entirely altered. The general government only has the power to treat with the Indian Nations, and any treaty formed and held without its authority will not be binding.

Here then is the security for the remainder of your lands. No state nor person can purchase your lands, unless at some public treaty held under the authority of the United States. The general government will never consent to your being defrauded. But it will protect you in all your just rights.

Hear well, and let it be heard by every person in your Nation, that the President of the United States declares, that the general government considers itself to be bound to protect you in all the lands secured you by the Treaty of Fort Stanwix, the 22nd of October, 1784, excepting such parts as you may since had fairly sold to persons properly authorized to purchase of you.

…Your great object seems to be the security of your remaining lands, and I have therefore upon this point, meant to be sufficiently strong and clear.

That in future you cannot be defrauded of your lands. That you possess the right to sell, and the right of refusing to sell your lands.

That therefore the sale of your lands in future, will depend entirely upon yourselves.

But when you may find it for your interest to sell any parts of your lands, the United States must be present by their agent, and will be your security that you shall not be defrauded in the bargain you may make.

The merits of Cornplanter and his friendship for the United States are well known to me, and shall not be forgotten. Remember my words Senekas, continue to be strong in your friendship for the United States, as the only rational ground of your future happiness, and you may rely upon their kindness and protection…. If any man brings you evil reports of the intentions of the United States, mark that man as your enemy, for he will mean to deceive you and lead you into trouble. The United States will be true and faithful to their engagements.

(The source of this letter is the *The Writings of George Washington* from the original manuscript sources, 1745-1799, prepared under the direction of the U.S. George Washington Bicentennial Commission and published by the authority of Congress. U.S. Government Printing Office, Washington; Vol. 31, Jan. 22, 1790–Mar. 9, 1792, pp.179-184, 1939.)

Somewhat on the sideline, but equally important to the Kinzua Dam, was the battle for water that developed between Pennsylvania and New York State. This was plainly evident in efforts to get the appropriations bill through Congress. New York State wanted the benefits derived from the storage and control of upper Allegheny waters. In short, it wanted to kill the Kinzua Dam project. They were in favor of an alternate project, the Morgan Plan, which would divert flood waters into New York State and Lake Erie.

Pennsylvania believed the water belonged to them—*it flows by way of Pittsburgh to the nation.* Thought was the water should be conserved, so its use extended through low water months, and it should be controlled in the spring as a protection to downstream residents.

There were deliberate attempts by New York congressmen to do more than stop the Public Works Bill. Their sights were trained directly on the proposed dam. Charles E. Goodell, of Jamestown, New York, was one of those working to thwart the Kinzua Dam project. Research revealed it was his lone vote that killed the Congress's effort to override Eisenhower's veto of the initial public works appropriation bill. He called the dam a pork barrel project, but the thought was he wouldn't describe it as such if the flood control project diverted the water of the Allegheny River to Chautauqua County, New York State.

The 1959 appropriations bill, which included money for early work in connection to Kinzua Dam, was but one example of political finagling related to the numerous appropriations of funds by Congress to implement projects authorized by the 1936, 1938, and 1941 Flood Control Acts.

It was not clear if the Kinzua funds would necessarily be cut out of the revised public works appropriation bill under development. There still remained unused funds for Kinzua Dam, $1,400,000, which were appropriated in the previous two years. Also, negotiations were already getting underway for obtaining land by agents of the U.S. Army Corps of Engineers, designers of the dam. Army engineers were also negotiating with the Pennsylvania State Highway Department for relocation of Route 59. The dam was not dead, but only delayed.

In September of the same year, 1959, Congress sent President Eisenhower another big public works appropriation bill containing the same projects which produced the veto of an earlier bill. All projects in the new bill were cut two and one-half percent.

The President vetoed this second public works appropriation bill. Unlike the first bill, the House voted this time to override President Eisenhower's veto on September 10, 1959. The House had never before voted to override an Eisenhower veto, but this time they had mustered the necessary two-thirds vote to pass legislation, despite the President's rejection of it.

The Senate followed the House action. The Senate vote to override was the first Eisenhower veto to be overridden. This was monumental. The bill provided $1,000,000 of old money and $1,365,000 of new money for the Kinzua Dam project. The latter sum represents $1,400,000 decreased by two and one-half percent, as provided in the revised bill.

Following the various federal budgets and congressional bills related to the Kinzua Dam would fill a volume or two by themselves—that is not the intent here. The message is clear and evident that politics played a major role in flood control in this country. This is particularly true for the Kinzua flood control project, as it involved not only the actions of American presidents and the American Congress, but the dishonoring of a treaty with the Seneca Indians, signed in 1794 by George Washington—the oldest treaty, incidentally, to which the United States is a party and which is still in force. The temperament of local, regional, and national politics was a foremost concern in the taking of land for Kinzua Dam.

The Congressional action giving the go ahead to proceed with the construction of Kinzua Dam was deplored by the President of the Seneca Indian Nation, George Heron. He spoke of the possibility that some of the Senecas would have to be forcibly removed from their lands in order to make way for the large Allegheny Reservoir.

Speaking in regards to the passing of the Public Works Bill, George Heron said in a letter, September, 1959, to the Associated Press:

> The recent action of Congress has brought much sadness to the Seneca. We must now leave our lands which we and our ancestors have cherished through all these years. It is ironical that in the Twentieth Century here in America that such a deed should again occur.

In his letter, Heron bitterly said he had hopes that in the future Congress would create a civilian agency to replace the U.S. Army Corps of Engineers.

> The problem of flood control and water conservation should be left to more learned men. The Army Engineers, of course, would retain the job of constructing pontoon bridges—a job to which they are more suitably adapted.

Over the years Congressional approval was given to the Corps of Engineers' plans for constructing numerous large reservoirs as flood control projects in the Allegheny-Ohio River Basin. In 1956, there were 10 dams in this flood control system. Eight of these dams affect Pittsburgh. They are the Tygart, Tionesta, East Branch (Saint Mary's), Mahoning, Crooked Creek, Conemaugh, Youghiogheny, and Loyalhanna. Two other dams, the Berlin and Mosquito Creek dams in Ohio, control the Mahoning and Beaver Rivers, and the Ohio below Pittsburgh.

Kinzua, still in the planning stage in 1956, was to be the number ten dam above Pittsburgh, Pennsylvania. The Conemaugh Dam, prior to Kinzua, was the largest in the system upstream from Pittsburgh. The Conemaugh was built at a cost of $48,000,000 and controls 1,351 square miles of watershed. Kinzua Dam controls 2,180 square miles of watershed.

Costs of building flood control dams are tremendous, but the amount of damage which they prevent can be even more startling. Costs of these nine dams, excluding Kinzua, were $114,710,000. The *Pittsburgh Press*, March 11, 1956, reported that existing dams on the Allegheny River had prevented more than $236,262,000 in flood damage. Without the dams, every time the rivers gained another foot over flood stage, the damage would climb by millions of dollars.

As a people, we have been slow to realize that water is part of our heritage. We attempt to purify it, control it, use it, and keep it. It can be the greatest natural asset possessed by a nation.

With the construction of Kinzua Dam, the increasing appreciation of the value of water was a new sign of the times in western Pennsylvania. Today this appreciation is being manifested all over the country as *rightful owners* dispute title to this prized natural resource.

ROCK DRILLS AND DYNAMITE

Perhaps this is our strange and haunting paradox here in America—that we are fixed and certain only when we are in movement.

- You Can't Go Home Again, Thomas Wolfe

The construction stage of Kinzua Dam required the purchasing of land and property from those situated in the areas involved. This included not only land for the actual dam and reservoir, but also land that was used for related purposes, such as recreation. Some property was also purchased because of alterations to highways, railroads, and utilities.

In 1959, the U.S. Army Corps of Engineers reported that land purchases would not be completed for at least two years. There was a promise to pay *fair market value*. The government planned to purchase land outright which was below the mean sea level elevation of 1,340 feet. This is the permanent reservoir level. It entered into easement agreements with landowners whose property was between 1,340 and 1,365 feet above sea level—1,365 feet above sea level being the high water level of the Allegheny Reservoir.

The very first purchase the Army engaged in was 216 acres at Big Bend, the immediate site of the dam. Purchasing of land upstream was governed by year-to-year appropriations of funds from the U.S. Congress. Fair market prices for property were established by real estate appraisers, either of the U.S Army Corps of Engineers staff or appointed appraisers, who then negotiated with property owners. To establish fair market value, the appraisers checked courthouse records and tax equalization files, which record market value and recent real estate sales of comparable property. When an agreement to sell could not be reached, the property involved came under condemnation proceedings by the government, which eventually resulted in a court ruling on the value of the property.

Condemnation proceedings for public projects did not include payment for indirect, incidental, and remote damages. These damages could include loss of goodwill a business had established, potential business profits, inability to purchase replacement property for the amount paid, and sentimental attachment. Little doubt remained among the landowners that there were unfair situations which developed. There have been legislative efforts since that time to change similar states of affair, to assure fair and adequate compensation for property condemned and seized by the government.

There were other incidental compensations due the property owner who was forced to relocate as a result of Kinzua Dam. The property owner could collect $6.25 an hour for time spent in search of a replacement site for his business or home and for travel time to that site. Compensation was limited to a maximum of fifty-six hours. The vehicle mileage allowance during the move was 5.5 cents per mile for a car and 7.5 cents per mile for a truck. Meal allowance was $1.00 a meal while traveling. These are 1960 dollar values.

Government land and property appraisers did not have an easy time with the New York State Seneca Indians. Simply put, relations were not good. The Indians had refused the appraisers entrance to their property. An effort by the federal government to reward the Indians in kind, by providing an equal amount of land elsewhere, was blocked by New York State, which would not agree to such an arrangement.

Some of the Seneca Indian farmers had done an excellent job of developing their reservation land. They were now faced with a unique problem—the land on a reservation does not actually belong to an individual, but belongs to the reservation. When reimbursements were made, a dispute could develop between the resident and the Seneca Nation of Indians. Who gets the money for improved and developed land? The farmer who invested his time, energy, and money felt aggrieved, and disputes needed to be settled—fast and equitably, as construction of the dam and reservoir was soon to get underway.

On Saturday, October 22, 1960, at 2:30 p.m., groundbreaking ceremonies for Kinzua Dam were held. An 18-car Pennsylvania Railroad excursion train with 1,400 passengers operated from Oil City, Pennsylvania, to the ceremony site at Big Bend on the Allegheny River. The *Bradford Era* newspaper, Bradford, Pennsylvania, reported this was the first passenger trip over the doomed railroad line in 30 years—as traffic had been limited to freight only.

October 22, 1960,
Groundbreaking
Cermony, above and
below. Left, last
passenger train from
Warren to Big Bend.

Among those attending the groundbreaking ceremony were Pennsylvania Governor David L. Lawrence and Senators Hugh D. Scott, Jr., and Joseph S. Clark, Jr. The Secretary of the Army, Wilber Bruckner, was the featured speaker. Bruckner compared the Army's work in such projects as flood protection with the Army's greater problem of protection of this country against the Communist threat. It seems that the Cold War permeated all political thought and most of the speeches of this era. The Secretary of the Army also said:

> This will be the largest reservoir in the authorized Allegheny-Monongahela Basin System. It will control some 2,180 square miles of this drainage area, approximately 19 percent of the entire Allegheny River Basin. Should there be a recurrence which caused the damaging floods of March, 1956, and January, 1959, in the Allegheny Basin, we calculate that the saving in flood damage because of this project would run well over $9 million. During the flood in March of this year, the project would have prevented damage estimated in excess of $7 million.

The following image shows attendees leaving the groundbreaking ceremony, as they receive the final *all-aboard* call for the last ride on this stretch of Pennsylvania Railroad line. The lower image is the Blanche Brownell farm, the future site of Kinzua Dam. One of the very first, of perhaps tens of thousands, survey stakes is seen in the lower right of the image. It marks the western end of the dam abutment.

Last passenger train departs Big Bend, groundbreaking, 1960.
Blanche Brownell farm, site of dam, survey stake, at lower
right, marks 1,375 ft. above sea level, the very top of the dam.

Dam construction, as well as relocation of the first three miles of Route 59 above the elevation of the dam's reservoir, soon began. This initial highway relocation extended from near Devil's Elbow, upstream from the dam, to a point across from the end of Dixon Island, downstream from the dam.

In August of 1961, a Quaker committee competed with the roar of giant earthmovers at the construction site in a *silent vigil* to protest the breaking of the 1794 treaty with the Seneca Indians. The Quaker group, known as the *Treaty of 1794 Committee,* was formed to point out the treatment of the Seneca Indians by the U.S. Government. Quaker honor was involved, as the Quakers had advised the Indians that the United States would stand by this treaty forever.

The Quakers now fervently believed that the U.S. Government committed the *unforgivable* in breaking the treaty with the Indians. Even though construction had been started, the *silent vigil* continued for three weeks, in hopes that construction would be halted. President Kennedy's letter to Basil Williams, then President of the Seneca Nation of Indians, even failed to seal the hopes of the *Treaty of 1794 Committee.*

The Kennedy letter outlined the policy being followed by the government with respect to the Kinzua Dam project. A copy of the 1961 letter was furnished by the Bureau of Indian Affairs (BIA), U.S. Department of the Interior, Washington, D.C., to Joseph H. Wick of North Warren, upon his request for information from the BIA relative to the Kinzua Dam project. It is part of the Wick archive of the Warren County Historical Society (WCHS), and the letter is presented here courtesy of Rhonda J. Hoover, Executive Director and Editor, WCHS.

> The White House
>
> Washington
>
> August 9, 1961
>
> Dear Mr. Williams:
>
> I fully appreciate the reasons underlying the opposition of the Indians to the construction of Kinzua Dam on the Allegheny River. Involved are very deep sentiments over a loss of a portion of the lands which have been owned by the Seneca Nation for centuries. I therefore directed that the matter be looked into carefully and that a report be submitted to me on the basic issues involved.
>
> I have now had an opportunity to review the subject and have concluded that it is not possible to halt the construction of Kinzua Dam currently under way. Impounding of the funds

appropriated by the Congress after long and exhaustive Congressional review, and after resolution by our judicial process of the legal right of the Federal Government to acquire the property necessary to the construction of the reservoir, would not be proper. Moreover, I have been assured by the Corps of Engineers that all the alternative proposals that have been suggested, including the so-called "Morgan Plan Number Six," have been thoroughly and fairly examined and are clearly inferior to the Kinzua project from the viewpoint of cost, amount of land to be flooded and number of people who would be dislocated. In addition, the need for flood protection downstream is real and immediate—the cessation of construction would, of course, delay the providing of essential protection.

Even though construction of Kinzua must proceed, I have directed the departments and agencies of the Federal Government to take every action within their authority to assist the Seneca Nation and its members who must be relocated in adjusting to the new situation. Included in the items I have directed the Executive departments and agencies to consider are (1) the possibility of the Federal Government securing a tract of land suitable for tribal purposes and uses contiguous to the remaining Seneca lands in exchange for the area to be flooded; (2) a careful review of the recreational potential resulting from the construction of the reservoir, and the manner in which the Seneca Nation could share in the benefits from developing this potential; (3) a determination of whether any special damages will be sustained because of the substantial proportion of the total Seneca lands to be taken; and (4) special attention and assistance to be given those members of the Seneca Nation required to move from their present homes, by way of counseling, guidance, and other related means. In the event legislation is required to achieve these objectives, I have asked that recommendations be prepared.

I hope you will convey to the members of the Seneca Nation the desire of the Federal Government to assist them in every proper way to make the adjustments as fair and orderly as possible. I pledge you our cooperation.

Sincerely,

/s/John F. Kennedy

The Kennedy administration had found it necessary, after careful consideration it reports, to continue with construction of the project. The President, however, had clearly recognized that acquisition of Seneca lands for the purpose of the Kinzua project required that special measures be taken to reduce detrimental impact on the Senecas. Statement that the Morgan Plan had been fairly examined was seriously questioned by the Seneca Nation of Indians and the competent engineers they had engaged. Efforts to stop the construction continued.

On December 28, 1961, opponents of the Kinzua Dam, in an attempt to halt construction which began in 1960, appeared on NBC-TV's *Today Show,* along with U.S. Government officials. Nearly one hour was devoted to the controversy associated with Kinzua Dam and the Allegheny Reservoir.

Opposing the project was Dr. Arthur E. Morgan, former chairman of the Tennessee Valley Association; Walter Taylor of the Friends Society Committee (Quakers); and George Heron of the Seneca Nation of Indians. Representing the U.S. Government's views and decision were Philleo Nash, U.S. Commissioner of Indian Affairs, and Major General William F. Cassidy, representing the U.S. Army Corps of Engineers. Nash stated that one of our obligations as citizens is to yield when the need arises, and he did not believe that there should be special rights for any group of citizens. The second half of the debate was heard the following day on the NBC *Today Show.*

Construction continued undaunted.

The Seneca Nation of Indians, as previously noted, had engaged the services of Dr. Arthur E. Morgan to suggest alternate proposals for the authorized Allegheny Reservoir as a means of providing flood control and low flow regulation on the lower Allegheny River. For over two years Dr. Morgan suggested variations of a scheme for diverting floodwater from the Allegheny River into a storage reservoir on the Conewango Creek, with provision for spilling water in excess of requirements for flow regulation into a channel discharging into Lake Erie.

INDIAN TRUTH, a publication by the Indian Rights Association, Philadelphia, Pennsylvania, having seventy-four years of non-partisan work for Indian civilization and citizenship to their credit, headlined the following:

> EMINENT ENGINEERS SAY KINZUA DAM NOT BEST
> METHOD OF FLOOD CONTROL—Arthur E. Morgan and
> Barton E. Jones, well known engineers, say the destruction of
> the homeland of the Allegany Seneca Indians is not necessary to
> control floods of the Allegheny River Valley.

Dr. Morgan and Mr. Jones were the engineers who planned and built the Miani Conservancy District (Ohio) of dams. Since 1914, it had made the Dayton Valley flood free. Dr. Morgan was President of TVA from 1933 to 1938. He and Mr. Jones had built the Norris Dam and 75 other major flood control projects.

In the *Pittsburgh Sun-Telegraph* Morgan declared:

> There is every indication that permanent and complete control of the flood waters originating in the Upper Allegheny River should be accomplished by diversion. The proposed diversion to carry the flood waters into Lake Erie would be approximately 41 miles long. It would be capable of safely handling a flood of 200,000 cubic feet per second, the largest ever recorded on the Upper Allegheny.

In summary, Dr. Morgan initially had five alternate proposals. The U.S. Army Corps of Engineers had engaged the firm of Tippetts-Abbett-McCarthy-Stratton (TAMS) "to study the engineering feasibility of such proposals as a basis for comparison with the authorized Allegheny Reservoir." Six months after the delivery of the TAMS engineering report in favor of the U.S. Army Corps of Engineers, Dr. Morgan presented his alternate Plan 6, which was thought to be the likeliest to gain approval.

All the Morgan Plans were rejected as being either more costly, or not meeting all the objectives as determined by the Corps, or "would not be controlling in obtaining a large factor of safety from floods at Pittsburgh," according to the U.S. Army Corps of Engineers. Dr. Morgan contended that the U.S. Corps of Engineers had in thirty years never seriously made an overall examination of any proposal other than their own. All alternate plans having been rejected, the U.S. Army Corps of Engineers confidently proceeded with their construction campaign.

The first portion of the Allegheny River Reservoir and Dam construction was completed by September, 1961. Beneath the relocation site for Route 59, very near the dam site, an entire hillside was excavated below the old road level and transferred across the river to the embankment site.

One-half million yards of earth, compacted on the former Blanche Brownell farm at Big Bend, formed the western abutment of the dam. From ground level at the embankment, the dirt was piled 140 feet high. The base is 950 feet long and

600 feet wide. The earth was sloped 45 degrees to an 18-foot width at the top. This top portion of the dam, when finished, would be utilized as a maintenance roadway.

Above, farming north of the village of Kinzua, 1960.
Below, Kinzua Dam construction, September, 1961.

In addition to planning for the new stretch of relocated Route 59, early excavation work got underway on the mountainside for the dam's eastern abutment. This required extensive digging down to bedrock. The first cofferdam was completed to protect this work, which was later to include construction of the concrete overflow, stilling basin, and sluice outlets of the finished dam.

The purpose of a cofferdam is to divert the river away from initial construction work. After the work is completed the cofferdam is removed. As work expands, additional and often larger cofferdams are required. The first cofferdam at the Big Bend site was considerably narrower than the second. The second cofferdam created a river only 80 feet wide, restricting the flow of the river and backing up water at times. The construction of the second cofferdam required the Army Corps of Engineers to purchase additional land—that now would be flooded in times of heavy rain.

Nearly half of the proposed $55 million budget for public works in Pennsylvania for the 1962–1963 fiscal year was earmarked for the Kinzua project in Warren County. $25,186,000 was scheduled for the eight-county district which contained the project.

Freight traffic on the Pennsylvania Railroad route from Warren to Olean via Kinzua officially ended August 1, 1962. This freight line had been in use twice a day. Pennsylvania Railroad received a $20,250,000 settlement from the U.S. Government for these 28.5 miles of line. The Pennsylvania Railroad abandoned this line beginning one-half mile downstream from the dam site.

Regular freight traffic had been discontinued, but the railroad line was not to be deserted entirely at this time. Now its sole purpose was to provide construction materials for the dam. In March of 1963, Hunkin-Conkey Construction of Cleveland, Ohio, began laying rail for their railroad system *within* the dam construction area. The firm installed a mile of railroad track within the work area.

Construction materials such as sand, gravel, and cement for Kinzua Dam were brought to the area by the Pennsylvania Railroad where Hunkin-Conkey had its own locomotive for switching purposes. This switching locomotive worked within the construction area of the dam. The Hunkin-Conkey locomotive brought cars loaded with construction materials off the Pennsylvania Railroad tracks nearby, onto company tracks for distribution in the work area.

During March of 1962, on the west bank of the Allegheny River, an aggregate unloading pit for railroad gondola cars was constructed in preparation for the production of concrete. Sand and gravel from rail cars were dumped into the pit, then conveyed through two large tubes to another conveyor system that carried the material to a batching plant. The sand and gravel required were shipped to the dam site in special, larger than normal railroad cars. At the batching plant the concrete for the dam was mixed.

In May of 1962, the erection of a 17,000-ton-capacity cooling plant was completed. This plant was used in the preparation of materials in the mixing of concrete. The cooling plant was one of the largest of its kind in operation at the time.

U.S. Army Corps of Engineers requirements stated that the concrete mixing materials needed to be between 40 and 50 degrees Fahrenheit during mixing and pouring operations. Normally it took between 30 to 45 minutes to cool the material to the required temperature, as a rule about 42 degrees Fahrenheit.

Four such facilities were erected to permit a continuous flow of material. The four 11-foot diameter tubes used to cool the material were 120 feet high. During concrete mixing operations about 16 yards were mixed at a time. Three four-yard-capacity railroad cars were used to haul the concrete to the site of pouring operations. The cooling plant was located on the west bank of the Allegheny River.

Operations of the cooling plant were controlled electronically on closed circuit television. A haul bridge was built at the dam. It was capable of supporting 160 tons and was traveled thousands of times by heavy earth-moving equipment. About 450,000 yards of concrete were used in the construction of the dam. Earth fill totaled about 3,000,000 yards.

The huge mixing and cooling plant provided concrete
for the dam. The batching plant had four mixers which
filled from above. Cooling towers were used to bring
the concrete mix down to the proper temperature. There
was a mile of railroad track within the worksite at the dam.
August, 1962.

Above, cofferdam construction on the east bank of the
Allegheny River, 1962. Below, trestle bridge is in place and
concrete monoliths are beginning to take shape, 1963.

With rock drills and dynamite, workmen bit into the rock formation along the east bank of the Allegheny River, where the Kinzua Dam is anchored or "keyed." At this time, February, 1962, workers were about sixty feet below the surface of Route 59, and about halfway to the river bed level. The Hunkin-Conkey Company workmen used caterpillar-mounted air hammers for this work.

Gantry cranes poured concrete for the main face of the dam.
These cranes set on a trestle that was 70 feet above the river.
The Gantry crane structure was also 70 feet tall, which
resulted in the crane operator being 140 feet above the
trestle base. The boom on each crane was 160 feet long with
each bucket pouring 10 tons of concrete per trip, 1963.

Workmen lay forms for the face of the concrete monoliths.
A total of 18 monoliths were required for the completion of
the concrete portion of Kinzua Dam, 1964.

Above, *Safety First* is urged as workers set forms for concrete on top of a monolith. Below, monolith #9, with two lower sluice gates completed, stands alone, 1965.

Upper and lower sluice gates completed, Kinzua Dam, 1965.

Kinzua Dam contains 18 monoliths. The six lower sluices of the dam are in monoliths eight, nine, and ten, with two lower sluices per monolith. There are also two upper sluices—one each in monolith seven and eleven. The two "box-like" openings at each side of the spillway are the high level sluices through the dam. They are identical to the six low level sluices through which waters of the Allegheny River flow. The sluices are 5 feet 8 inches wide and 10 feet in height.

Tainter gates are specialized gates installed across the top of the dam spillway. Each tainter gate is a huge semi-circular steel prefabricated unit—24 feet high and 45 feet wide. Four of the tainter gates span the 210-foot gated section at the top of the concrete portion of the dam. Regular flow of water will pass through the 8 sluice gates, which can each pass more than 100 cubic feet of water per second. The tainter gates are used for excess runoff from the reservoir. After the tainter gates were installed, the 18-foot-wide service road was constructed across the top of the dam.

The dam is designed for a flood peak flow of 151,000 cubic feet per second. Prior to construction, maximum flow recorded at the site of the dam was 60,500 cubic feet a second in March, 1956, a year of record floods. There is enough concrete in the spillway section of the dam to build a 300-mile, two-lane highway. The earth and rock portion of the dam represents 300,000 trips to the site by 20-ton trucks.

In the following July, 1963, image you can only speculate what the dialogue was between the U.S. Army Corps of Engineers resident geologist, Fred DeGroskey, and the unidentified woman—and who will be the first to resort to use of the bull horn found on the ground between them! Meanwhile, giant dump trucks, dwarfed in size by the dam, continued to work relentlessly.

Unidentified woman airing her opinions to a geologist. Below, a 20-ton truck moving stone fill at the dam site.

Early March of 1964, it was discovered that a seepage condition existed in the west bank or earthen portion of the dam. Immediate attention was needed. Halsey Harmon, project engineer, explained that the porosity of native gravel deposits allowed the seepage. The gravel deposits on the west side of the dam had built to great depths over the years. This was a natural occurrence.

The concrete portion of the dam was built where substantial foundation bedrock could be reached. As part of the construction process, holes were drilled deep into bedrock below this portion of the dam, and concrete was forced into them under pressure to fill any cracks or fissures caused in part by the tremendous weight of the dam.

The concrete portion of the dam is not entirely solid—there exists control and inspection tunnels within the concrete. These form a 4000-plus-foot network of passageways that enable dam workers to go to any of the control devices if they become inoperative.

The earthen portion of the dam was built upon the deeper gravel deposits—not directly on bedrock. The Corps described the seepage condition in this portion as not dangerous, just unfortunate. Corrective measures were called for.

May 27, 1964, it was announced that the firm of Icanda, Ltd., Montreal, Canada, had been awarded a $2.3 million contract to build a cutoff wall that would correct the seepage condition.

On the earthen portion of the dam, the Icanda contract called for the construction of a cement wall that would descend through the depths of the gravel and into bedrock to a depth of two and one-half feet. At points, the wall would reach depths of 175 feet. The wall would be three feet thick.

The method used by Icanda, Ltd., to pour the wall was a patented method or process. This firm was one of only six that specialized in this type of construction. Kinzua Dam was the first time this patented process was used in the United States. It successfully resolved the problem.

Final clearing of the reservoir area continued. Buildings had been razed, trees timbered, and debris burned, but some large bridges still remained. In early 1966, workmen of the Cuyahoga Wrecking Company of Cleveland, Ohio, placed six huge pontoons beneath a section of the Pennsylvania Railroad Bridge that crossed the river in the vicinity north of the dam.

When the pontoons were in place the water level within the reservoir was raised to float the disengaged sections of the bridge free. These sections were then towed toward shore and beached on dirt dikes constructed for this purpose. Then the structures were cut into junk lengths.

Three sections of the bridge and two trusses were removed from the river in this manner. Once removed, the Army Corps of Engineers allowed the water level to the dam to be raised permanently. This procedure was also used on the former Route 59 bridge in the village of Kinzua. Flood waters in late February of 1966 hampered this salvage operation, making the work difficult and dangerous.

Above, Pennsylvania Railroad Bridge at Tuttletown, a short distance upriver from Big Bend. Below, aerial view of the same bridge with old Route 59 clearly visible, 1957.

With project completion approaching, the huge tube that once fed materials to the concrete mixing plant needed to be disassembled after the last pour. The mixing plant also was torn down to make way for the proposed Kinzua Hatchery, a fish-rearing facility to be built immediately below the dam. Gone, too, was the haul bridge within the basin of the Kinzua Dam. It had served its purpose and was removed to make ready for the backup of the river water.

Upon completion of the dam, the Pennsylvania Railroad track was also completely abandoned. The rail in the 28.5-mile track was salvaged, but the railroad bed remained as it was.

Also nearing completion was the relocation of the second stretch (Step 2) of Route 59 between Warren and Marshburg, Pennsylvania. The relocation of Route 59 had three major steps. The first step began a little more than 3 miles south of the dam and proceeded northward to Devil's Elbow, between the town of Kinzua and the dam. Step 2 of the relocation of Route 59 stretched approximately 9.5 miles from the Marshburg area toward the town of Kinzua. Step 3, the final step, was the building of Casey Bridge.

Casey Bridge, nearly half of a mile long, spans a portion of the Allegheny Reservoir near the mouth of Kinzua Creek. The opening of Casey Bridge completed the largest of the highway relocations in Pennsylvania made necessary by the Kinzua Dam and Allegheny Reservoir.

Casey Bridge construction for relocated Route 59.

The bridge was constructed by the John F. Casey Company of Pittsburgh. It was engineered by a former Kane man, Frank G. Sciullo, of Westmoreland Engineering Company, Vernon, Pennsylvania. The 4.5 million dollar contract was awarded on February 21, 1963.

The Casey Bridge had rivaled the Kinzua Dam itself as a sightseer attraction during construction. Its length is 1,819 feet. It contains 6,200,000 pounds of steel and rises 171 feet from the Kinzua Creek. At reservoir full level, 1,365 feet above sea level, as much as 140 feet of water runs under the bridge, inundating the Kinzua Valley. The 1,365 level is predicted to be reached once every 50 to 100 years. Normal summer pool level is 1,328 feet above sea level, which would place 90 to 100 feet of water under the Casey Bridge.

Concrete pillars await steel as construction on the Casey
Bridge continues. Below, the old swinging bridge across the
Kinzua Creek stands as a reminder of slower times in the valley.

The Casey Bridge is completed, all 1,819 feet of it. Below, the stark beauty of deep winter demands acknowledgement.

In a flurry of activity, the Kinzua Dam project was finished by late summer, 1966. A huge dedication ceremony, attended by an estimated 3,000 people, was held on September 16, 1966.

A quote from the Dedication Program reads:

> The Allegheny Dam and Reservoir is a monument to man's engineering skill. It is a tribute to the spirit of cooperation among men that made it possible. It is a memorial to the sacrifice of peoples and communities who moved to make way for its waters. To all of us, it is an investment in the future of this country.
>
> Viewing the Allegheny Dam today we see concrete, steel and earth fashioned by a variety of skills into a structure with both practical and aesthetic values. We see it here and now, but its effect is far-reaching and extends more than 2,000 miles to the Gulf of Mexico where its summer discharge will help retard the intrusion of salt water into the Mississippi River at New Orleans.
>
> In partial operation over the 1965-1966 flood season, it is credited with prevention of flood damages estimated at $1,700,000. This is a dividend over and above the benefits to accrue from its operation in the decades ahead.
>
> As we dedicate this project to its intended use in the service of mankind, we conclude another step in the effort to improve the environment wherein succeeding generations must flourish.

Dedication ceremony was held on September 16, 1966, above.
Kinzua Beach is seen left of Casey Bridge, marina is on the right.

Kinzua Dam, 1979, is shown with the two upper sluice gates wide open. This creates significant whitewater disturbance in the dam's stilling basin.

In August of 1959, President Eisenhower had before him a bill authorizing construction of a fish hatchery in northwestern Pennsylvania. The intent was for the hatchery to stock the huge reservoir of the not-yet-begun Kinzua Dam and other waterways for fishermen from Erie and Pittsburgh, Pennsylvania; Buffalo, New York; and Cleveland, Ohio. Final legislative approval came with Senate passage of the bill—estimated cost of the hatchery was $2.5 million. Hatchery construction began soon after the dam was completed.

It was thought that heavy fishing by sportsmen on regional waterways after the dam was completed would create a need for an additional hatchery. A small federal hatchery at Farnsworth, east of Warren, Pennsylvania, had been closed by the government in 1965. Today, the Farnsworth Fish Hatchery functions on the support and efforts of volunteers. It was expected that when recreation was developed thousands would flock to the vicinity of the reservoir, as the dam would be within a few hours driving distance from several major cities.

Above, the fish hatchery from the west side of Kinzua Dam.
Below, the fish hatchery from the east side, overlooking the
stilling basin of the dam.

It was planned that the hatchery would start its own fish from eggs, but not strip its own eggs. The eggs would be brought in from a disease-free station for rearing in the Kinzua facility.

The original reason for placing the hatchery near the dam was to take full advantage of the favorable water of the reservoir. The water supply for the hatchery would be taken from the reservoir at different elevations in order to obtain desirable temperatures for hatchery purposes. This plan was soon to be abandoned.

Since the fish would be distributed not only to the Allegheny Reservoir, but to streams throughout the Allegheny National Forest and elsewhere—there was concern over disease. It was decided that water from wells drilled 70 to 80 feet deep at the site would be used to flow through the hatchery raceways rather than water pulled directly from the Allegheny Reservoir. Reservoir water was to be used only in an emergency, due to its greater potential for the spread of disease. There are pipes through the dam that can be used as an auxiliary water supply for the hatchery.

The individual raceways at the Kinzua hatchery are 80 feet in length, clustered in five lengths per unit. They are 8 feet wide, double raceways with dividers in the middle. Initially four of these 400-foot-long double raceways were constructed.

The plan was that five hundred miles of streams in the Allegheny National Forest were to be served by the Kinzua hatchery. This encompasses four counties: Warren, Forest, Elk, and McKean. The hatchery also serves western portions of New York and Pennsylvania, as well as northern parts of West Virginia.

While stocking the reservoir, there was a mass escape. In this Kinzua mix-up, the fugitives were nearly three-quarters of a million large mouth fingerling bass that the Interior Department's Bureau of Sports Fisheries and Wildlife had stocked in the upper Allegheny Reservoir in June, 1966. The escapees simply swam downstream through the open dam gates—contrary to the bureau's original intention.

The straying fish were the result of a slip-up in the coordination of activities of the Army Corps of Engineers and the Bureau of Sports Fisheries and Wildlife, which wanted to make the new man-made lake a paradise for sportsmen.

The engineers had closed the gates to the dam to build up the summer's recreational pool to about 1,240 feet above sea level. This was sufficient for the bureau's fish-stocking project, and the fish were dropped by air as had been planned.

The U.S. Army Corps of Engineers, forgetting about the recently stocked fish, treated the newly created summer recreational pool of the reservoir as only a temporary event. A few weeks after stocking the bass fingerlings the engineers opened the dam's gates, drastically reducing the elevation of the pool to about the level of the old riverbed. This was done as part of a necessary project to clean out logs and other debris that had collected against the upriver side of the dam.

The logs were cleaned out, but so were most of the fish that swam downstream!

The following spring the Interior Department's Bureau of Sports Fisheries and Wildlife—not ones to be easily discouraged and with tax-payers' dollars in hand—stocked the reservoir with one million bigmouth bass, five million walleyed pike, and 50,000 muskies. The dam, having stabilized the flow of the Allegheny River, now provides many miles of suitable trout habitat immediately below the dam. The reservoir also soon grew into favorable fish habitat, and is presently visited by many eager anglers.

On New Year's Day, 2003, a record breaking northern pike was caught on the Allegheny Reservoir. A Bradford, Pennsylvania, man was ice fishing and landed the 35-pound fish, which measured 48 inches in length and 21 ½ inches in girth. The Pennsylvania Fish & Boat Commission verified it as a record. The previous state record was caught in the Allegheny Reservoir too, 23 years ago. That pike weighed 33 pounds and 8 ounces.

A concern arose that there was all this water flowing from the dam and not a kilowatt of energy was being made from it. Initially the Army Corps of Engineers did extensive studies on the possibilities of power generation at Kinzua Dam and reported that the annual average river flow did not justify the cost of a conventional hydroelectric installation.

Studies did reveal, however, that the small power potential of the Allegheny River could be utilized if coordinated with a pumped-storage project. This type of project, it turns out, only becomes economical when it can be tied into a large electrical grid, such as the one Penelec maintained with other electric utilities. Penelec was the local supplier and distributor of electricity for consumers in the region.

Cleveland Electric Illuminating (CEI) Company and the Pennsylvania Electric Company (Penelec) applied jointly to the Federal Power Commission in Washington, D.C., for the license to construct and operate a proposed $40 million pumped-storage generation plant at Kinzua Dam. CEI and Penelec agreed to pay the federal government an annual fee for use of the water, the dam, and federal lands. Construction began on the Seneca Power Plant in April, 1966, and the plant was completed in 1969.

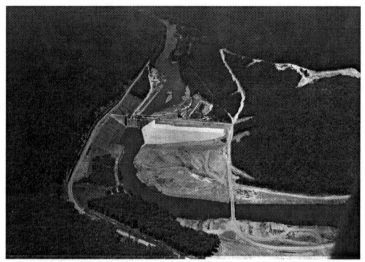

Part of the the Allegheny National Forest, incredibly dense
and vast, is seen above, 1965, and below, 1967. The immense
Kinzua pumped-storage reservoir is in the foreground, below.

It seems this major construction project attracted so many *sidewalk superintendents*, asking so many questions, that safety became an ongoing issue on the site. People were repeatedly asked not to cross construction lines or enter into the work areas. A *quick facts* brochure was produced by Penelec and CEI to encourage cooperation among those overly eager to watch the unique construction process. Some of the facts from that brochure are:

> The Seneca Power Plant, a pumped-storage hydroelectric plant, contains five major elements: a water intake structure behind the dam; two 15-foot diameter steel pipes from the intake structure, through the dam, to the powerhouse; the powerhouse, housing two reversible pump-turbines, each rated at about 175,000 kilowatts of generating capacity, and one non-reversible turbine of about 30,000 kilowatts capacity; a 22-foot diameter, steel and concrete lined tunnel extending into the mountain for a half-mile; and an upper reservoir for water storage.
>
> Water behind the dam provides the lower pool for the power plant. This water is drawn into the powerhouse through two 15-foot diameter pipes extending through the dam from the intake structure on the upriver side. The pumped-storage reservoir covers some 100 acres to a depth of 64 feet. It is located atop a mountain 800 feet above and a half-mile from the power plant.

Above, flooding at Grass Flats on the Allegheny River, just
west of Warren, PA. Such early 20th century flooding was an
annual event that the building of Kinzua Dam put to rest.

Below, a winter view of the reservoir with ice, March, 1970.

Essentially, with the huge water reservoir uphill from the dam, this facility stores the ability to generate large quantities of electricity for later use. The plant installed two 175,000 kilowatt reversible pump-turbines, which were a relatively new development at the time, for both pumping water and generating electricity. During low power demand periods, electricity drives the reversible turbines as pumps lift the water from the reservoir up 800 feet to the upper reservoir.

When peaks in power demand occur, water stored in the upper reservoir can be released, generating electricity as it falls through the same turbines which pump it up hill. Instead of flowing downriver after generating power, as is the usual case, most of the water is sent back into the Allegheny Reservoir behind the dam from which it came. In addition, the Kinzua plant installed a 30,000 kilowatt conventional hydroelectric turbine, to operate from water in the upper reservoir to generate additional electricity. The non-reversible turbine operates only during periods of water discharge.

During the generating operation, one of the reversible turbines returns all discharged water only to the reservoir behind the dam. The other reversible unit discharges either behind the dam or downriver, in keeping with the Army Corps of Engineers river flow requirements. The non-reversible unit only discharges downriver.

What is distinctive in this variable discharge feature of the Seneca Power Plant is that much of the water will be used over and over to generate power. When the Allegheny Reservoir storage must be conserved, the power plant returns all water, except a minimum specified release, to the Allegheny Reservoir storage. When a large downriver discharge is desired, the power plant discharges a large amount of water downstream. The Corps of Engineers reports that there is no significant temperature variation, which could be harmful to fish life and the Allegheny River.

Above, the water intake on the north side of the dam is under construction for the power plant. Below, the finished power plant is seen just to the right of the dam's spillway.

Operations at Kinzua Dam were very good for the next several years, but in 1973 severe corrosion of the stilling basin's concrete floor had been detected. The condition was caused by heavy gravel and sizable stones being agitated within the confines of the stilling basin. This agitation was caused by the dam's turbulent discharges of water. This situation was considered normal in dams as large as Kinzua. As it was thought that any delay would only add to the cost of the eventual repairs, it was decided to proceed with the repair work in July.

The project called for the construction of a cofferdam at a midway point in the stilling basin, with a closing at the end to connect to the east bank of the river. Stabilizing materials such as clean sand and gravel were trucked to the site to eliminate any need to disturb the river's natural bottom.

The cofferdam was pumped dry and holes that had been gouged in the stilling basin were filled with a dense concrete mix. This was followed by the placing of a 12-inch thick overlay of concrete reinforced with steel fibers over the entire basin floor. The steel-fibrous overlay employed provided a far greater resistance to abrasive action than normal concrete.

The stilling basin neutralizes the force of water coming through the dam by a system of baffles. Repairing and reinforcement of the baffle piers was also accomplished. This first phase of the repair project was finished in November, 1973.

The second phase of the project, a duplicate procedure on the west side of the stilling basin, was started in July of the following year and completed in November. The Corps reported that downstream water quality was not affected. There was no contractor dredging, no disposal of reinforced materials in the river, and no disturbance of the river's bed reported.

The following diagram illustrates the dam's spillway section profile where the 1973–1974 stilling repairs took place. Shown separately are the embankment profiles of the concrete and earth embankments, and sea level elevations in feet of the various seasonal pool levels. The length in feet of the various dam components is illustrated lastly.

These measurements are from Army Corps of Engineers documents. Documents researched from different decades show the overall reported length varying by a few feet; apparently, means and methods of measurement by man obviously varied over the decades.

KINZUA DAM

Maximum base widths:
Concrete section, 195 feet
Earth embankment, 1050 feet

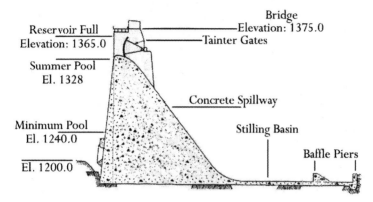

Spillway Section Profile

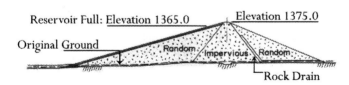

Embankment Profile

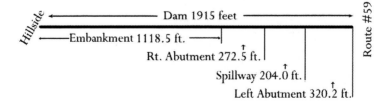

Above, new Route 59 is seen running parallel to the reservoir. Below, the Allegheny Reservoir is full. Power station is located to the right, and the fish hatchery is seen to the left of the dam.

TOURISM AND RECREATION

Travel, in the younger sort, is a part of education; in the elder, a part of experience.

~ Sir Francis Bacon

The common prediction was that Kinzua Dam, object of controversy and debate for decades, would become a major tourism attraction. The people of the upper Allegheny River Valley, a valley that had sent lumber and oil to the world by way of the river, hoped that unprecedented prosperity would result from Kinzua Dam and the Allegheny Reservoir; and that the prosperity would be of a much more lasting nature than that derived from the lumber and oil booms of the past.

In 1959 the Warren County Development Association (WCDA), promoter of economic growth and economic development in Warren County, went on record by adopting a formal resolution urging Congressional approval of funds to enable the U.S. Army Corps of Engineers to proceed as soon as possible with planning and construction of the Kinzua Dam project. The resolution was directed to the Appropriations Committee of the U.S. House of Representatives.

The WCDA endorsed the project as a means of preventing flood damage and repeated disruption to industry. The development group also stressed the importance of Warren County's existing resort and tourist industry. The group stated:

> Preliminary reports from our constituents have confirmed the Association's view that the dam will have a very beneficial effect upon the development of the county as a major recreation complex.

In 1960, when actual construction was initiated, Kinzua Dam was within 300 air miles of 50 million people. Statistics from the 1960 census report indicated a population of approximately 586,000 within a 50-mile radius of the reservoir. The 50-mile radius was considered an *immediate area*, and was selected as such since only one hour's driving time would be required to reach the Allegheny Reservoir. Studies from the 1960s anticipated that the greater portion of annual visitation to Kinzua Dam would be made by people living beyond this immediate area.

On a regional basis, the Allegheny Reservoir is centrally located with several highly urbanized areas within a 130-mile radius. The 1960 census reported a population of over 11 million living within a regional 130-mile radius, including Cleveland, Pittsburgh, and Buffalo. The 1950 and 1960 census figures for these three cities respectively are: Cleveland, 1,465,500 and 1,786,700; Pittsburgh, 2,213,200 and 2,392,100; and Buffalo, 1,089,200 and 1,301,600.

While these cities were growing in population during this time, it was also being recognized by analysis of the census numbers that the population growth in the typically rural counties and townships of northwestern Pennsylvania had been generally zero for decades. Many communities had once been larger than they were in 1960, according to census statistics. This was particularly true for the small settlements to be affected by the Kinzua Dam. For example, the population of Kinzua Township in 1940 was 541; in 1950 it was 485; and in 1960 the population was

458. A similar pattern holds true for Corydon Township: 1940, population 260; 1950, population 263; and 207 in 1960. Of course, who would build a home or business in an area rumored to be doomed by the construction of a dam—rumors heard in these Allegheny hills as early as the 1930s.

Following the peak of petroleum production, which occurred in the early 1890s, Warren County developed as an important agricultural and dairy farm center. The 1960 census reported over 1,200 farms with an average size of 131 acres. Also at that time, major manufacturing industries in the county ranged from steel fabrication to plastics to electronics plants. Tourism and recreation had taken a back seat in the county's economics—its future potential remained uncertain.

The following figures are interesting to consider. The Allegheny National Forest records indicate that over 315,000 hunters and fishermen visited this forest for an average of 1.5 days each during the year 1956. In an article, *Deer Economics*, in the *Pennsylvania Game News*, January, 1956, J.K. Pasto and D.W. Thomas record that the typical deer hunter spent an average of $36.00 during the hunting season. If it is then projected that 30,000, or less than ten percent of those hunters and fishermen, spent their time and money in Warren County, then over a million dollars would have flowed into the coffers of Warren County businesses in 1959. Granted, the accuracy of such predictions may be shaky, but it is obvious that the flow of significant dollars into the region is a distinct possibility, if tourism and recreation were properly pursued and developed.

According to a 1960 report issued by the United States Department of Agriculture, recreational demands within the National Forest lands in the Allegheny Reservoir area would produce the following projected attendance figures: 1966 attendance of 735,000; 1976 attendance of 1,530,000; and 2000 attendance of 3,750,000. The 1960 report stressed that these projected figures were conservative in view of past trends and in consideration of the growing increase in all types of water-based recreation. For example, according to the National Association of Engine and Boat Manufacturers, there was an increase from 2.5 million pleasure crafts in the U.S.A. in 1947 to 7.3 million in 1958.

In 1960 all bets were on tourism and recreation. The conclusion was that it was obvious from all the data that the Allegheny Reservoir would have the potential for becoming the leading recreational facility in the region—and becoming the leading industry in the county of Warren. How was Warren County to fully realize this great potential? This was the bottom line.

One disadvantage the County Planners had at the time was the fact that they were not certain of the amount of land and the exact location of the land to be acquired by the U.S. Army Corps of Engineers, or what additional lands were to be acquired by the National Forest Service. The Allegheny National Forest then encompassed 472,000 acres owned outright by the U.S. Government. The area was divided almost evenly among four counties of northwestern Pennsylvania. Its care was, and still is, administered by the Forest Service of the U.S. Department of Agriculture.

Access to the reservoir was an additional problem. In one early 1960s Warren County Planning Commission report concerned with access to the reservoir, the physical characteristics of the Allegheny Reservoir were compared to the fiords of Norway and Sweden—that is, steep, tree-covered banks running down to the water's edge, with occasional inlets and bays created where major creeks and streams feed into the main reservoir. Generally speaking, the inlets and bays are where the existing topography permits access to the reservoir. Today, evidence of this can be seen at Willow Bay and Wolf Run Marina. Compare this to nearby Chautauqua Lake in New York State where the topography around the entire lake perimeter is such that it can be developed for public and private usage—and has been extensively. Many slopes around the Allegheny Reservoir are extremely steep, with grades in excess of 25 degrees and in some instances more than 45 degrees. The western shore of the reservoir is a special problem in regard to public access, as roads are minimal.

In July of 1962, the Warren County Planning Commission's report, *A Time for Action*, emphasized that:

> Much has been said and written concerning the potential of the Allegheny Reservoir as a recreation facility and the impact it will have at a county, state, and even national level. While these studies are informative and useful, the fact remains that the most affective controls for proper development can only be adapted and administered at a local level—in this case, the townships.

While it is reasonable and judicious to be inclusive of all levels of government when doing such planning, it may be unrealistic to expect efficient administration on the township level, beyond assuring that proper zoning is in place. Certainly, the development for a land area covering multiple counties and crossing into two states needs comprehensive plans that could be adapted and administered on a regional basis—not by the townships. There was a distinct need for comprehensive planning.

In April of 1964, a long-awaited Bureau of Outdoor Recreation report was released by the Secretary of the Interior, Stewart L. Udall. The report recommended that a national recreation area NOT be established around the reservoir because the area would stop at the New York State line and would not have a national character. The Allegheny National Forest does not extend into New York State.

Also, it was recommended in the Bureau of Outdoor Recreation report that the federal lands around the reservoir be developed for recreation under the administration of the U.S. Forest Service. The U.S. Army Corps of Engineers would regulate discharge from the reservoir. The Corps would also cooperate with the federal Fish and Wildlife Service and the Pennsylvania Fish Commission in the rearing and stocking of trout and in management of the fishery resources.

According to Forest Service analysis the following projects would be accomplished in the next 15 years—that is, by 1980: facilities for boat launchings, swimming, camping; sightseeing and observation points; trails and nature studies; marinas and boating services; food services and supplies; lodging; and sports. Recreation would be broadened to all seasons, including a winter sports area to extend the stay of tourists. The Allegheny National Forest prediction was clear—recreation would be big business.

In April of 1965, a transfer of funds in the amount of $450,000 from the Corps of Engineers to the U.S. Forest Service enabled the staff of the Allegheny National Forest to plan, program, and design recreation areas at Sugar Run, Kinzua Point, Wolf Run, and Dew Drop.

In 1966, Warren County was expecting potentially significant economic returns from recreation due to Kinzua Dam and the Allegheny Reservoir. Talk was that recreation could become the largest single contributor to the income of Warren County. The amount of such income, and therefore Warren County's well being and prosperity, was directly dependent upon the wise and controlled use of the land surrounding the reservoir.

An article about the attractions of the Kinzua Dam area was published in June of 1966, in the *New York Times* Sunday Travel Section. The article noted that the construction and completion of the Kinzua Dam, the breaking of old Indian treaties, and the expropriation of the lands granted to Cornplanter and his heirs forever, added a romantic aura to the technical wonders of the dam itself. Without a doubt, those families who lost their homes failed to experience this *romantic aura.* Colonel Henry C. Kerlin, of the Warren Chamber of Commerce at the time, observed that the *New York Times* story was one more indication of how hot a tourist attraction the region had become.

In the third quarter of 2003, the Allegheny National Forest Service published in the Federal Register a notice of intent to revise its Forest Plan. Four preliminary issues explored in preparation of the new plan were: special area designation; recreation; vegetation management; and habitat diversity.

Presently, one of the more controversial concerns the Forest Service faces involves the designation of more wilderness areas on the Allegheny National Forest, but the most frequently debated item may well be an issue of the previous 1986 Forest Plan. That concern was a call for a motel-restaurant complex to be built with private funds on the Allegheny Reservoir, possibly close to the Wolf Run Marina and Kinzua Beach area.

An October 9, 2003, quote from the Forest Service in a general announcement regarding the revision of the Forest Plan said:

> The motel-restaurant complex adjacent to Kinzua Beach has not been constructed. Comments received from recent public meetings in regard to Forest Plan revisions indicate there is a division of interest with some people wanting to see the resort constructed while others do not. The controversy remains unchanged.

The Forest Service intends to look at whether the overall need for recreational development along the Allegheny Reservoir has been met. The Forest Service stated that since the 1986 Forest Plan was first adopted:

> User preferences have changed. For example, where hunting may have been a lead recreational activity in the past, today's activities include more variety and focus on a wide array of opportunities such as hiking, biking, sightseeing, wildlife viewing, fishing, boating, horse riding, driving for pleasure, ATV riding, and hunting.
>
> Changes are needed to meet the public demand and avoid user conflicts and to address the capability of the Allegheny National Forest to support the activities.

Currently, the Forest Service has ten campgrounds of varying sizes available in the Allegheny National Forest that surrounds the immediate area of the reservoir. Different facilities are available at the campsites. Five campsites suitable for trailers and motor homes, as well as tents, are available. Five other campsites are accessible only by hiking or boating. Of these latter sites, several provide stopover points while hiking on several loop trails or the larger North Country Trail.

Six boat launches within the National Forest, in addition to the Kinzua-Wolf Run Marina, provide access to the waters of the Allegheny Reservoir. Aside from several very scenic picnic areas, there are also two beaches for swimming—the larger beach being near the Casey Bridge and Wolf Run Marina.

The shoreline of the summer pool level on the reservoir is 91 miles, of which 63 are in Pennsylvania and 28 are in New York. When busy, the facilities of the Forest Service seem rather sparse to serve 63 miles of shoreline. The navigable water—summer pool—also provides access to 22.5 miles of the Allegheny River within the National Forest. The reservoir provides navigation in the Kinzua Creek, 10 miles; Sugar Run, 3.3 miles; and Willow Creek, 2.3 miles. The extent of this recreation area is 450 square miles or 288,000 acres.

In the Forest Plan under development, the Forest Service says it intends to examine recreation as it relates to timber, oil, and gas development. Road building is another important issue. Revisions to the 1986 Forest Plan, which will address all these issues, are expected to be adopted by the U.S. Forest Service by 2006. The new Forest Plan will be the primary management tool for Allegheny National Forest use over the following ten to fifteen years.

Three specific items add to the difficulties facing the Forest Service in its development of plans for tourism and recreation. First is the obvious fact that the Allegheny Reservoir spans two states: Pennsylvania and New York. Think of this as one side of a tourism triangle.

The second side of the triangle is the fact that nearly the entire portion of the shoreline of the Allegheny Reservoir in Cattaraugus County, New York State, is bounded by the Allegany Indian Reservation of the Seneca Nation of Indians. The Seneca Nation of Indians provides for camping, cabins, and boat launches; but no extensive facilities are available.

Approximately 20,000 acres of Allegany Reservation land are available for whatever purposes the Seneca Nation desires. About 10,000 acres, the most productive land, was lost to the waters of the reservoir. Much of the remaining area is characterized by narrow, hilly strips of land situated between maximum flood-pool elevation and the reservation boundary. In the New York section of the reservoir, the Seneca Nation has exclusive control of land access to the summer pool. It also holds legal title to the land under water, subject to flowage easement. When the reservoir is at its low level, the land at the northern end is nothing more than mud flats awaiting the return of the high water level.

The third side of this tourism triangle is Allegany State Park. It contains 65,000 acres, which include major recreation areas and many scenic opportunities for outdoor recreation. Allegany State Park is east of the Seneca Indian Reservation and completes the Allegheny River oxbow portion *(See Map 1.)* of the upper reaches of the Allegheny River.

Surrounding this unwieldy triangle are dozens of municipalities, townships, and counties, all wanting—and needing—to compete for tourism dollars. This is a large and complex geographical area with more than its share of political and economic challenges.

An additional anomaly on the Allegheny Reservoir is the Onoville Marina. It is located on the western shoreline of the Allegheny Reservoir in New York State. This area is leased to Cattaraugus County by the U.S. Army Corps of Engineers. It is a very popular summer spot and offers 400 plus docks and mooring spaces, a campground, and picnic facilities.

Above, the Allegheny Reservoir as seen from Jake's Rocks. Below, Kinzua Dam, the pump station reservoir, and the very dense and extensive Allegheny National Forest, 1970.

The development of a comprehensive, far-reaching plan for tourism and recreation on the Allegheny Reservoir is no straightforward matter; but it is likely that the Kinzua Dam will be the centerpiece for future development of recreation in the Allegheny National Forest—and part of that centerpiece may very well be a resort.

The concept of a resort at Kinzua received little negative reaction before it was incorporated into the Forest Service Plan in 1986. The resort concept has been vehemently opposed since the plan was finalized, particularly in 1990 by the *No Kinzua Resort Coalition* based in Warren, Pennsylvania. The intent of this coalition was to preserve the reservoir just as it is—according to the coalition a resort would only detract from the reservoir. Of course, in 1990 the reservoir had been *just as it is* for only twenty-five years, but the battle lines had been drawn.

In the 1986 Forest Plan the Forest Service thought there was a need to develop overnight accommodations—the better the accommodations, the easier it becomes to attract people from greater distances. Despite the plan's statement of need, opposition to the resort was strong. At a congressional hearing held in Pittsburgh in 1989, public comments ran 82% against the resort development on the Allegheny Reservoir.

All efforts to create a Kinzua Dam and Allegheny Reservoir resort have failed—no resort has materialized, though numerous heated debates have occurred. Another round of similar conflict is certain, as the new Forest Service Plan is projected to be completed by 2006.

In January of 2003, the Seneca Nation of Indians opened a Las Vegas-style casino in Niagara Falls, New York. Shortly after this opening the Seneca Nation announced that they could possibly open a casino on the Allegany Reservation in the next five years—perhaps near Salamanca, New York. The 2003 idea of an Allegany Reservation casino was updated by the Seneca Nation in January of 2004—it now appears likely that the construction of a casino in or near Salamanca may begin early in 2004—four years sooner than originally projected.

Salamanca has the distinction of being the only city in the United States that completely sets on an Indian reservation. It is located on the northern extremity of the Allegheny Reservoir. Its origin is in the mid-nineteenth century, when the Erie and Pennsylvania Railroad bought land rights and established a railroad junction on the Allegany Reservation. This site grew into a village named Hemlock, but was renamed later for Don Jose Salamanca Mayel, a large stockholder in the Erie and Pennsylvania Railroad. In an 1875 federal statute, Congress authorized long-term leasing of reservation land, in what was loosely called *congressional villages*—including the city of Salamanca and five other villages which had grown up within the reservation.

During the opening of the casino in Niagara Falls, Seneca Nation officials discussed the future of gaming. Cyrus Schindler, former Seneca Nation President and Seneca Niagara Falls Gaming Corporation chairman, confirmed that in the near future a casino may be built near Allegany State Park and Salamanca.

A vote of the Seneca people would need to be held before a casino could be built on Seneca Nation tribal lands. Ricky Armstrong, Seneca Nation President in 2003, acknowledged that the people needed to support any proposed casino. Armstrong anticipated that the required vote regarding a Salamanca-area casino would be forthcoming. Each casino constructed bankrolls the construction of the next casino.

The Seneca have the authority to build up to three casinos in western New York based on a contract with the state. Buffalo, New York, has also been mentioned as a potential casino site. Casinos remain a controversial issue, but many communities desperately need the jobs and tax dollars generated by a casino.

The Salamanca area is being eyed for a casino because of its proximity to ski resorts and summer recreation areas, including Kinzua Dam and the Allegheny Reservoir. Studies done by the Seneca Nation have shown that gaming enthusiasts will travel to casinos. Clients would be drawn from Erie, Pittsburgh, and Cleveland. The potential for economic development based on casino openings is appealing to many, but it remains highly divisive to the general population.

Today, Kinzua Dam remains a controversy on several fronts. After the terrorist attacks of September 11, 2001, security was greatly increased at Kinzua Dam. The dam was viewed by the federal government as a potential site for future attacks by terrorists. Increased security was accomplished in a very low profile manner—public tours on and inside the dam were stopped, boating and fishing near the dam and its tailwaters were curtailed, and visitors were more carefully scrutinized. Security for the dam was not the only concern, as the power station and its pumped-storage reservoir are a vital part of the region's power grid.

During the 2003-2004 Christmas and New Year's holidays, the federal government heightened the nation's terror threat level to "orange," indicating a high risk of terrorist attacks. Due to the higher level of risk of terrorism the December 23rd *Warren Times Observer* newspaper ran a front page story regarding increased vigilance in the county. The image which accompanied this headline was a background picture of Kinzua Dam with a large orange bulls-eye in the foreground with the words, "Bravo Plus."

At this time, the U.S. Army Corps of Engineers, which is responsible for operations at the dam, raised its security level to "Condition Bravo-Plus," as the country started the 2004 New Year's celebration. There are four general levels of military security: Alpha, Bravo, Charlie, and Delta. The highest level of security is Delta. Operations at the dam were adjusted in response to this increased threat level with little comment from Corps officials.

In January, 2003, the *Readers' Forum* column of the *Warren Times Observer* carried several references to the dam and reservoir. A state-of-the-art E-911 system in a slated courthouse addition was planned as part of a $5,000,000 Bond Fund approved by the Warren County Commissioners. Objections arose, as the E-911 system was to be installed in the path of potentially raging waters, should the Kinzua Dam fail structurally. What good would an emergency response system do in the immediate path of a potential disaster, such as a failed dam? Nearly a half-century after construction was completed, the dam still weighs heavily on the minds of some who live below it along the banks of the Allegheny River—and most likely, always will.

As Warren County, home of Kinzua Dam, faces growing financial problems and increased taxes on every front, an individual in a 2003 *Readers' Forum* column lamented the decline of taxable property—a good portion of Warren County being tax-exempt due to the Allegheny National Forest. The Allegheny National Forest, created in 1923, now contains 513,000 acres. This particular writer to the *Forum* was also deploring the *unscrupulous government bureaucrats* who remove property from tax rolls at the expense of the tax-paying public. The property referenced that was removed from the tax rolls in this case consisted of the homes, businesses, and farms taken by the government for construction of Kinzua Dam and the Allegheny Reservoir—bitter feelings of resentment exist decades after the government's taking of property by eminent domain.

Tourism and recreation are especially relevant topics in Warren County today, as the decline of the manufacturing sector continues its downhill spiral. Major manufacturers were lost in the first years of the new millennium. Long-standing companies in the community, such as National Forge Company and Loranger Manufacturing, entered bankruptcy proceedings and closed their doors. In January, 2004, Blair Corporation, one of Warren County's largest employers, announced the closing of their national outlet store in Starbrick, Warren County. Outlet sales held a unique place in Blair's retailing history for three decades. Prior to their outlet store, Blair held annual week-long warehouse sales at the Warren headquarters. Shoppers would flock to Warren and wait in line on the sidewalk, often all night, to be among the first to buy the deeply discounted goods. While Blair maintains their corporate headquarters in Warren County, the closing of the Starbrick outlet will hamper efforts to attract tourists. The popularity of the outlet with its warehouse bargains had maintained it as a regular stop for tourist buses—so much so, that many establishments referenced their location according to whether they were east or west of the Blair outlet.

The first-ever United States Canoe Association (USCA) national canoe and kayak championships in Warren County were held in July of 2003. This 5-day event featured the main race starting at the Kinzua Dam and progressing down the Allegheny River to Warren. Rains had been heavy and the river was very high, but efforts were made by the U.S. Corps of Engineers to accommodate the national races by optimizing dam outflow as much as possible. There were over 400 participants from 37 states and Canada—and one paddler from Australia. Warren County will again host the national championship in 2005. The USCA is working on the event to cater to recreational paddlers as well as those interested in a national competition.

Also in July, 2003, the annual Kinzua Classic Bike Race was held with nearly 180 cyclists participating. Cyclists were from Pennsylvania, New York, Ohio, and other states. The 30-mile course ran from Kinzua Beach, just across the Casey Bridge on Route 59, to Jake's Rocks and back to Kinzua Beach. The elite class of cyclists negotiated the course twice for a total of 60 miles, while regular competitors pedaled it once.

The September, 2003, issue of *National Geographic Adventure* recognized the Allegheny River as host to one of the nation's *40 Great Fall Weekends*. This was in reference to a canoe renter's 30-mile trip from Kinzua Dam to Tidioute, with overnight camping on one of several islands, part of the Allegheny River Island Wilderness. The community of Tidioute, about 25 miles downriver from the dam, is rated as one of the best fishing locations in the East. Hundreds of fishermen gather for the annual state championship fishing contest. Part of the billing for the Allegheny River canoe trip said:

> Float some of the remotest waters in Pennsylvania, 30 miles from Kinzua Dam to the town of Tidioute. Make camp under sycamore and silver maple on one of the eleven wilderness islands.

The company providing the service is Allegheny Outfitters, Warren, Pennsylvania. Without a doubt, canoe trips such as this provide a taste of the wilderness that first attracted explorers to this expanse of heavily forested land, where the black bear still roams. The forest holds deer, wild turkey, and today bald eagles may again be seen soaring above the tree line as you float the river.

The upper Allegheny River was never neglected by fishermen, hunters, and lovers of its natural beauty; but they kept it to themselves. Construction on the dam attracted many new visitors to the area, which had been almost unknown to tourists. Past efforts to sustain tourism have not been sufficient, but today new direction is being provided by the Northern Alleghenies Vacation Region (NAVR). Funding to promote tourism is slowly improving; for example, a new 3,600-square-foot NAVR visitor's center is currently under construction in Starbrick, just west of Warren. It will open in 2004, under guidance from the NAVR director, Diane Shawley, who fought long and hard to establish this new visitor's center in the heart of Kinzua country.

Warren County Commissioners instituted a bed tax, essentially a tax on tourism, in 2002. This is a three percent tax implemented on rooms at hotels, motels, and bed-and-breakfast lodging in the county. From July 1, 2002, through June 30, 2003, this new tax generated $80,701. Two percent of the tax goes into the county coffers for administrative fees. This is new revenue and will allow NAVR to promote tourism in ways it never could before the tax was implemented. The tax revenues will allow the agency to expand the venues to which it markets the county as a place to visit and stay. It is predicted that it will take at least three years before county tourism officials will know how consistent the bed tax funding will be from year to year.

Tourism is the second largest industry in Pennsylvania. It creates jobs, generates tax revenues, and offers opportunities for business growth. It has emerged as the new hope for economic revitalization.

EPILOGUE

EPILOGUE

There is an assertion that the Allegheny River in northwestern Pennsylvania was the southern limit in this area of immense ice sheets from the last ice age. Geologists will tell you that by studying this region of the Allegheny River much can be learned of the conditions of the previous ice age—the Allegheny always having told an interesting story. There is geological verification that the Allegheny had previously been two rivers—one river flowed southwest along the present course from Big Bend, and then flowed north either at the Conewango Creek or took the northern course as far away as French Creek at Franklin, Pennsylvania. The second river, also originating at Big Bend, flowed in the opposite direction—north and east. It ultimately reached Lake Erie a few miles east of present-day Dunkirk, New York. Big Bend, site of Kinzua Dam, was the point of origin for these two rivers. As the glaciers retreated and erosion occurred, the Allegheny carried the detritus, ice, and snow—outwash from the great glacier—as swiftly as nature allowed. The ridge at Big Bend, which separated the two Alleghenies, was eventually worn through. The Allegheny River then slowly assumed its present course to the Ohio River, the Mississippi River, and onward to the Gulf of Mexico. The U.S. Army Corps of Engineers was evidently aware of the geological uniqueness of Big Bend. The Corps, in a sense, restored what nature had torn asunder.

Time and man—from Cornplanter to the Corps of Engineers—have continually transformed the Allegheny River valley. Tremendous changes have occurred. In truth we cannot deny what the early settlers and the Seneca have produced for us. The likes of Cornplanter, Handsome Lake, Philip Tome, the early Quakers—all those who first made this area home—established the strength and character upon which we build today.

Burke, poet of the Seneca, wrote:

> The Long House knows the passage of the sun
>
> Over the sewn bark from its Eastern Door
>
> To where the hidden trails all westward run
>
> Beyond the Gen-nis-he-yo Gahunda's roar,
>
> Beyond the Tu-ne-wan-da and its marches
>
> Beyond the hill-bound Allegheny stream,
>
> Beyond the Ni-aga-ra, and the washes
>
> Of blue O-hee-yo where the sunset gleam,
>
> Glories the sailing of the white canoe

Driven beyondward by the Indian soul

Forth from the dawn of living to the new

Enduring dawn. Upon the eternal scroll

Time writes the passing…and unto the last

The Long House throws its shadows on the vast.

The future of the valley of the upper Allegheny River was predetermined in the 1930s with talks of flood control. As time drew nearer for construction of Kinzua Dam, even the last protesters conceded their world was doomed. It was not the end of the world, but it was the end of their world, their way of life—for how can you infuse hope into the spirit of man when all is ordained to be taken from him?

To those who intimately knew these times, perhaps the valleys are better known by what is gone than by what remains today. True, the past cannot be captured, but we may forever ponder the times lost—villages abandoned; farms without green fields; trees cleared and burned, as the fires set by the Corps rid the valleys and remote hamlets of the residue of human life.

For centuries the Allegheny hills acted as stewards guarding, perhaps falsely, the destiny of the inhabitants. Kinzua Dam held back the river as everyone and everything previously known vanished beneath it. As some witnessed the extinction of a valley, others marveled at the engineering of a great dam—for as Cornplanter discerned—*upon the eternal scroll, time writes the passing.*

GLOSSARY

GLOSSARY

Brodhead, David–American general who ascended the Allegheny River from Pittsburgh into the Seneca land in northwestern Pennsylvania and southwestern New York as part of a three-prong attack against the Seneca. Clinton and Sullivan attacked from the north and east to complete this military campaign.

Burke–Seneca poet.

certiorari–a writ of superior court to call up the records of an inferior court or a body acting in a quasi-judicial capacity.

Chenussio–the western most of the Seneca people, those associated with the Genesee and upper Allegheny Rivers, as opposed to the Seneca of the Finger Lake region of New York State.

Clinton, James–Revolutionary War general who campaigned with Sullivan against the Iroquois Nation, specifically the Seneca and Cayuga in the scorched earth march of 1779.

Cofferdams–water-tight enclosures that prevent water from washing the concrete away as it is poured. Water is diverted to permit construction.

Conudiu–Quaker rendering of Ganioda-yo, Handsome Lake.

Cornplanter, Chief–Seneca variously known as John Abeel, John O'Bail, Gy-ant-wa-chia, "By What One Plants," and Ki-on-twog-ky.

Deardorff, Mearle H.–At the time of the Adoption Ceremony of Governor James, Mr. Deardorff was President of the Warren County Historical Society and the Chairman of the CORNPLANTER INDIAN COMMITTEE of the State Federation of Historical Societies. He co-sponsored the Adoption Ceremony.

Fallen Timbers, Battle of–near Toledo, Ohio, 1794, convinced western tribes to end their resistance to expanding white settlements. Cornplanter's efforts to cultivate peace and friendship between the Western Indians and the U.S. Government were not successful, but he kept the Iroquois from joining the Western Indian Rebellion which was crushed at Fallen Timbers.

Ga-in-dah-qua–"She Picks Up the Plants," Alice White of the Wolf Clan.

Gaiwiio or Gaiweeyoh–the "Good Word" or "Good Message" of Handsome Lake, the Seneca prophet.

Ganiodayo–also found as Ganiodaio, Ganyotaiyo, or Skaniadariyo, meaning: "It is a Very Large Lake" or "It is a Handsome Lake." Handsome Lake, older half-brother of Cornplanter by a common mother. Conudiu is the Quaker rendering of Handsome Lake's Seneca name.

Ga-wa-so-wan-neh–Dr. Arthur C. Parker, Seneca Indian, was New York State archaeologist, and director of the Rochester Municipal Museum.

Great Law of Peace–an unwritten law of conduct of the Iroquois Confederacy that was created to bring peace to all Iroquois nations.

Gy-ant-wa-chia–Cornplanter's Seneca name, meaning "One Who Plants" or "By What One Plants."

Ha-gao-ta–Johnny Cash's Seneca name, meaning "Story Teller."

Haudenosaunee–Iroquois, the "People of the Longhouse."

Jenuch-Shadega–Junishadago or Jennesedaga, village of Chief Cornplanter on his land on the Allegheny River.

Jonh-Ya-Dee–Jimersontown, one of two Seneca Indian relocation communities in New York State. The second community is Steamburg.

Kinzua–"Place of Many Fishes," sometimes "Fish on Spear." Corruption of Seneca word, genzo, meaning "Fish Up There."

Kiasutha–Seneca leader and maternal uncle of Cornplanter.

Moiety–Seneca clans are traditionally divided into two groups of four clans. These groups are called moieties. One moiety consists of the Wolf, the Turtle, the Bear, and the Beaver. The other moiety consists of the Deer, the Heron, the Snipe, and the Hawk.

Morgan Plan–an alternate flood control project to divert excess water from the upper Allegheny River to Lake Erie through the Conewango basin of western

New York, named after Dr. Morgan who was retained as a consulting engineer by the Seneca Nation of Indians. Dr. Morgan gained international recognition as the first chairman of the Tennessee Valley Authority (TVA). In earlier years he drafted drainage engineering codes which were enacted by five states as law. As president of Antioch College, Yellow Springs, Ohio, from 1920 to 1936, Dr. Morgan shaped America's first large scale regional planning program and directed construction expenditures of $200,000,000 while with the TVA.

O-Dahn-Goht–Seneca name, which means "Sunlight," given to Governor James at his Adoption Ceremony.

Oleeguh-Hannah–Seneca name for Allegheny River.

Oswego–a small trading post on the southern shore of Lake Ontario, where in July of 1777, a majority decision was made by the Iroquois Nations to join England in the war against the colonies.

Perfidy–a breach of faith, treachery, disloyalty. The Allegheny Reservoir is sometimes referred to as Lake Perfidy due to the breaking of the Treaty of 1794 by the government of the United States.

Planters Field–home to Cornplanter Town on the mainland of the Cornplanter Grant.

Red Jacket–fiery and eloquent Seneca orator, who opposed Cornplanter's cooperation with the whites, particularly Cornplanter's ceding and sale of large areas of Seneca land in western Pennsylvania and New York to the Americans.

Rock barrow–quarry, on top of the hill on the west bank of Allegheny River, above the Kinzua Dam construction.

Sachem–A member of the ruling council of the Iroquois Confederacy.

Sagoyouwatha–"He Who Keeps Them Awake," Red Jacket, Iroquois Chief, who generally held the white man in contempt as the power of his nation declined. He was a patriot, who was known for his fearless eloquence in denouncing enemies.

Sandford Plummer–noted Seneca artist of Gowanda, New York, who created Governor James' adoption scroll.

Seneca Clans–Wolf, Turtle, Bear, Beaver, Deer, Heron, Snipe, and Hawk.

Skaniadariyo–Handsome Lake, half-brother to Cornplanter. It was on the Cornplanter Grant that Handsome Lake had his visions, which resulted in the initiation of a "New Religion" among the Iroquois.

Sluices–gates built into dams to allow the outflow of water.

Steamburg–one of two Seneca Indian relocation communities in New York State. The second community is Jimersontown.

Sugar Run Mound–archaeological site on the Pearl Smith farm in Warren County. Pennsylvania Historical and Museum Commission reports: "No intimate connection can be traced between 'Mound-builders' of Sugar Run and the Cornplanter band or the other Senecas living just across the line in New York State." This site, at the mouth of Sugar Run, revealed burial mounds and a village of Hopewellian Indian culture.

Sullivan, John–Revolutionary War general who campaigned with Clinton against the Iroquois Nation, specifically the Seneca and Cayuga in the scorched earth march of 1779.

Tainter Gates–specialized gates installed across the top of the Kinzua Dam spillway. Each tainter gate is a huge semi-circular steel prefabricated unit–24 feet high and 45 feet wide. Four of the tainter gates span the 210-foot gated section. Regular flow of water passes through the 8 sluice gates. The tainter gates are used for excess runoff from the reservoir.

Thirteen Fires–a poetical reference to the original thirteen states of the new Republic. From the Indian point of view a "fire" meant a tribe or an Indian nation, which maintained its own council fire.

Treaty of 1794–the oldest treaty to which the United States is a party and which is still in force, a treaty signed by George Washington–also known as the Canandaigua Treaty of 1794 and the Treaty of 1795.

Treaty of Paris–treaty of peace between Great Britain and the United States, officially ending the Revolutionary War and recognizing the independence of the United States, signed September 9, 1783, Paris, France.

Tsonondowanenaka or Tsonondowaka–Senecas, "People of the Great Hill or Mountain."

Wayne, Anthony–American General, who in 1794, defeated the Ohio tribes with finality at the Battle of Fallen Timbers. Cornplanter kept the Seneca and other Iroquois Nations out of this conflict.

APPENDIX

Seneca Reservations

Kinzua Dam Fact Sheet

The Preamble of the Canandaigua Treaty of 1794

Directions to Riverview Cemetery

SENECA RESERVATIONS

1. **Allegany Indian Reservation**–The Allegany Indian Reservation is located along the Allegheny River from the Pennsylvania border upriver to Vandalia, New York, and is located entirely within Cattaraugus County. It is approximately 1.6 miles wide and 29 miles long. The reservation originally included 30,469 acres of land surrounding the Allegheny River, of which some 10,000 acres were inundated by the Kinzua Reservoir when the Army Corps of Engineers built the Kinzua Dam. This reservation also includes the City of Salamanca. Villages included within the Allegany Indian Reservation include Onoville, Quaker Bridge, Red House, Kill Buck, Carrollton, and Vandalia.

THE SENECA NATION OF INDIANS
G.R. Plummer Building
PO Box 231
Salamanca, New York 14779

2. **Cattaraugus Indian Reservation**–The Cattaraugus Indian Reservation is located along the Cattaraugus Creek, from Gowanda, New York, downstream to the shore of Lake Erie. The reservation is comprised of some 21,618 acres in Cattaraugus, Chautauqua, and Erie counties.

THE SENECA NATION OF INDIANS
William Seneca Building
1490 Route 438
Irving, New York 14081

3. **Oil Springs Indian Reservation**–The Oil Springs Indian Reservation is located on the border of Cattaraugus and Allegany counties near Cuba, New York. This reservation is made up of one square mile of land that includes access to Cuba Lake. Although the Oil Springs Reservation has no permanent Seneca residents, there are Seneca Nation and privately owned enterprises operating on the reservation.

DAM FACTS

Kinzua Dam and the Allegheny Reservoir are located eight miles north of Warren, Pennsylvania, and 198 miles north of Pittsburgh. Nineteen percent of the entire Allegheny-Monongahela basin system is controlled by Kinzua Dam. Its purpose, as stated by the U.S. Army Corps of Engineers, is flood control, navigation, power, pollution abatement, and recreation.

A total of 1,280 properties were acquired for construction of the Kinzua Dam. Other items acquired were: 36.7 miles of railroad; 60 miles of highway; 80 miles of power lines; 66 miles of communication lines; 38 miles of pipeline; two schools; nine churches; 13 cemeteries; 50 businesses; 495 homes and 385 cabins.

The volume of concrete used in the dam was 500,000 cubic yards. The volume of earth fill was 3,000,000 cubic yards. The maximum base width in feet for the concrete section is 195 and the maximum base width in feet for the earth embankment is 1,050 feet.

The land under the full pool level or the 1,365 feet above sea level is as follows: 644 acres of the Cornplanter Grant, 1,604 acres of the Allegheny National Forest, and 7,516 acres of private land in Pennsylvania. Under water in New York State are 10,000 acres of the Seneca Allegany Reservation, 84 acres of Allegany State Park, and 1,317 acres of private land.

The Kinzua Dam, from stream bed to crest is 179 feet high and 223 feet from the foundation to crest. It is 1,915 feet long and is a concrete cavity spillway flanked on the west by an earth-filled embankment. The drainage area above the dam is 2,180 square miles or 1,395,200 acres.

The minimum pool is 1,240 feet above sea level; winter pool, 1,292; summer pool, 1,328; full pool, 1,365. The top of the dam is 1,400 feet above sea level.

The permanent (minimum) pool is 40 feet deep at the dam. It inundates 1,700 acres and floods 7.7 miles upstream. The summer pool is 128 feet deep at the dam; it extends over 11,400 acres, flooding 27.7 miles. The full pool is 165 feet deep at the dam and will flood 34.7 miles of river and create a 20,700-acre lake. There is a total shoreline of 91 miles, 63 of them in Pennsylvania. Navigable water readings are: Allegheny River, 22.5 miles; Kinzua Creek, 10 miles; Sugar Run, 3.3 miles; Willow Creek, 2.3 miles.

In 1963, Colonel De Melker of the U.S. Corps of Engineers stated the frequencies at which the Corps expects the various elevations of the Allegheny Reservoir. The Corps expects the 1,328 elevation up to an elevation of 1,330, or 2 feet above the summer pool level, at least once annually. The Corps expects to reach 1,335, or 7 feet above the summer pool, once every 2 years. The Corps expects to reach elevation 1,340 once every 5 years. And they expect to reach elevation 1,344 once in ten years; and elevation 1,350, or 15 feet below reservoir full, once in 25 years.

De Melker further pointed out that the Allegheny Reservoir would not have been expected to be filled during their period of record keeping. U.S. Army Corps of Engineers records go back to 1865, that is, intermittent records, records of major storms. The Corps has continuous records since the early 1900s. From these records it was determined that the maximum elevation that any storm would have produced was elevation 1,354, or 11 feet below reservoir full.

Hurricane Agnes, 1972, brought the Allegheny Reservoir elevation to within a couple feet of the 1,365 reservoir full level. This was a new record.

The Allegheny River covers a mere 135 miles as the crow flies, but has actual shoreline of more than 325 miles in length. Its path twists and meanders so greatly that *old timers* report that there is not a point on the compass to which it does not direct its course. The Allegheny River, most likely named by the Seneca, meaning "Fair Water"—the French named it La Belle Riviere, or "Beautiful River."

PREAMBLE OF THE CANANDAIGUA TREATY OF 1794

The Seneca Nation of Indians
The Canandaigua Treaty of 1794
Preamble of the Canandaigua Treaty

A Treaty Between the United States of America and the Tribes of Indians Called the Six Nations:

The President of the United States having determined to hold a conference with the Six Nations of Indians for the purpose of removing from their minds all causes of complaint, and establishing a firm and permanent friendship with them; and Timothy Pickering being appointed sole agent for that purpose; and the agent having met and conferred with the sachems and warriors of the Six Nations in general council: Now, in order to accomplish the good design of this conference, the parties have agreed on the following articles, which, when ratified by the President, with the advice and consent of the Senate of the United States, shall be binding on them and the Six Nations....

ARTICLE 1. Peace and friendship are hereby firmly established, and shall be perpetual, between the United States and the Six Nations.

ARTICLE 2. The United States acknowledge the lands reserved to the Oneida, Onondaga, and Cayuga Nations in their respective treaties with the State of New York, and called their reservations, to be their property; and the United States will never claim the same, nor disturb them, or either of the Six Nations, nor their Indian friends, residing thereon, and united with them in the free use and enjoyment thereof; but the said reservations shall remain theirs, until they choose to sell the same to the people of the United States, who have the right to purchase.

ARTICLE 3. The land of the Seneca Nation is bounded as follows: beginning on Lake Ontario, at the northwest corner of the land they sold to Oliver Phelps; the line runs westerly along the lake, as far as Oyongwongyeh Creek, at Johnson's Landing Place, about four miles eastward, from the fort of Niagara; then southerly, up that creek to its main fork, continuing the same straight course, to that river; (this line, from the mouth of Oyongwongyeh Creek, to the river Niagara, above Fort Schlosser, being the eastern boundary of a strip of land, extending from the same line to Niagara River, which the Seneca Nation ceded to the King of Great Britain, at the treaty held about thirty years ago, with Sir William Johnson); then the line runs along the Niagara River to Lake Erie, to the northwest corner of a triangular piece of land, which the United States conveyed to the State of Pennsylvania, as by the President's patent, dated the third day of March, 1792; then due south to the northern boundary of that State; then due east to the southwest corner of the land sold by the Seneca Nation to Oliver Phelps; and then north and northerly, along Phelps' line, to the place of beginning, on the Lake Ontario. Now, the United States acknowledge all the land within the aforementioned boundaries, to be the property of the Seneca Nation; and the United States will never claim the same, nor disturb the Seneca Nation, nor any of the Six Nations, or of their Indian friends residing thereon, and united with them, in the free use and enjoyment thereof; but it shall remain theirs, until they choose to sell the same, to the people of the United States, who have the right to purchase.

ARTICLE 4. The United States have thus described and acknowledged what lands belong to the Oneidas, Onondagas, Cayugas and Senecas, and engaged never to claim the same, not disturb them, or any of the Six Nations, or their Indian friends residing thereon, and united with them, in the free use and enjoyment thereof; now, the Six Nations, and each of them, hereby engage that they will never claim any other lands, within the boundaries of the United States, nor ever disturb the people of the United States in the free use and enjoyment thereof.

ARTICLE 5. The Seneca Nation, all others of the Six Nations concurring cede to the United States the right of making a wagon road from Fort Schlosser to Lake Erie, as far south as Buffalo Creek; and the people of the United States shall have the free and undisturbed use of this road for the purposes of traveling and transportation. And the Six Nations and each of them, will forever allow to the people of the United States, a free passage through their lands, and the free use of the harbors and rivers adjoining and within their respective tracts of land, for the passing and securing of vessels and boats, and liberty to land their cargoes, where necessary, for their safety.

ARTICLE 6. In consideration of the peace and friendship hereby established, and of the engagements entered into by the Six Nations; and because the United States desire, with humanity and kindness, to contribute to their comfortable support; and to render the peace and friendship hereby established strong and perpetual, the United States now deliver to the Six Nations, and the Indians of the other nations residing among them, a quantity of goods, of the value of ten thousand dollars. And for the same considerations, and with a view to promote the future welfare of the Six Nations, and of their Indian friends aforesaid, the United States will add the sum of three thousand dollars to the one thousand five hundred dollars heretofore allowed to them by an article ratified by the President, on the twenty-third day of April, 1792, making in the whole four thousand five hundred dollars; which shall be expended yearly, forever, in purchasing clothing, domestic animals, implements of husbandry, and other utensils, suited to their circumstances, and in compensating useful artificers, who shall reside with or near them, and be employed for their benefit. The immediate application of the whole annual allowance now stipulated, to be made by the superintendent, appointed by the President, for the affairs of the Six Nations, and their Indian friends aforesaid.

ARTICLE 7. Lest the firm peace and friendship now established should be interrupted by the misconduct of individuals, the United States and the Six Nations agree, that for injuries done by individuals, on either side, no private revenge or retaliation shall take place; but, instead thereof, complaint shall be made by the party injured, to the other; by the Six Nations or any of them, to the President of the United States, or the superintendent by him appointed; and by the superintendent, or other person appointed by the President, to the principal chiefs of the Six Nations, or of the Nation to which the offender belongs; and such prudent measures shall then be pursued, as shall be necessary to preserve our peace and friendship unbroken, until the Legislature (or Great Council) of the United States shall make other equitable provision for that purpose.

NOTE: It is clearly understood by the parties to this treaty, that the annuity, stipulated in the sixth article, is to be applied to the benefit of such of the Six Nations, and of their Indian friends united with them, as aforesaid, as do or shall reside within the boundaries of the United States; for the United States do not interfere with nations, tribes or families of Indians, elsewhere resident.

IN WITNESS WHEREOF, the said Timothy Pickering, and the sachems and war chiefs of the said Six Nations, have hereunto set their hands and seals.

Done at Canandaigua, in the State of New York, in the eleventh day of November, in the year one thousand seven hundred and ninety-four.

TIMOTHY PICKERING

Witnesses
Israel Chapin, Wm. Shepard, Jun'r, James Smedley, John Wickham, Augustus Porter, James H. Garnsey, Wm. Ewing, Israel Chapin, Jun'r

Interpreters
Horatio Jones, Joseph Smith, Jasper Parrish, Henry Abeele

(author's note: Signed by fifty-nine Sachems and War Chiefs of the Six Nations.)
CANANDAIGUA, NEW YORK - NOVEMBER 11, 1794

DIRECTIONS TO RIVERVIEW CEMETERY*

Directions to Riverview Cemetery *from* Warren, Pennsylvania, are as follows:

- Take Route 6 east to Route 59.
- Follow Route 59 past Kinzua Dam to Route 321.
- Turn left onto Route 321.
- Follow Route 321 north to the intersection of Route 346. The abandoned Corydon General Store will be on the right.
- Take Route 346 west.
- At the New York State border, Route 346 becomes Route 280. From there, turn left on the first road in New York State. This road is unmarked, but will take one directly to the Riverview Cemetery. If the road is gated, park and walk on the road approximately one-tenth mile to the cemetery.

* Riverview Cemetery received remains from earlier graves at Corydon Cemetery, the Cornplanter Grant, and areas of the original Riverview Cemetery that were flooded by the waters of the Allegheny Reservoir. The dead were exhumed and reburied at the expanded Riverview Cemetery. The new Cornplanter Monument may be viewed at Riverview.

BIBLIOGRAPHY

Adoption Ceremony Report
Cornplanter Grant
Warren County, Pennsylvania
August 24, 1940

The Allegheny River
S. Kussart
Burgum Printing Company, 1938

The Allegany Senecas and Kinzua Dam: Forced Relocation Through Two Generations
Joy Ann Bilharz
Lincoln: University of Nebraska Press, 1998

Atlas of Warren County, Pennsylvania, 1878
Howden and Odbert
Reprinted by the Warren County Historical Society, 1995

Big Damn Foolishness: The Problem of Modern Flood Control and Water Storage
Elmer T. Peterson
Devin-Adair Company, 1954

Chief Cornplanter, a Memorial Biography
On the Occasion of the Pilgrimage of the Society to the Home and Tomb of Cornplanter, July, 1926
Erie County Historical Society Publications Vol. 1, No.1
Erie County Historical Society, Erie, Pennsylvania, 1926

Cornplanter, Can You Swim?
Alvin M. Josephy, Jr.
American Heritage
Volume XX, Number 1, December, 1968

The Cornplanter Grant in Warren County
Merle H. Deardorff
The Historical Society of Western Pennsylvania
Reprinted from the *Western Pennsylvania Historical Magazine*, Volume 24, Number 1, March, 1941

Corydon-In Remembrance
Ruth Tome Funk
Edited and compiled by Ruth Prue Burgett, neice of Ruth Tome Funk, 1980

The Death and Rebirth of the Seneca
Anthony F.C. Wallace
Knopf, 1970

Evidence of Things Unseen
Marianne Wiggins
Simon and Schuster, 2003

A Flood Control Dam for the Upper Allegheny River, Forty Years of Controversy
A Case Study in the Politics of Flood Control
Roy E. Brant
A thesis presented to the faculty of the Department of Political Science, West Virginia University, 1969

A Friend Among the Senecas, the Quaker Mission to Cornplanter's People
David Swatzler
Stackpole Books, 2000

Halliday Jackson's Journal to the Seneca Indians, 1798–1800
Edited by Anthony F.C. Wallace, (Pennsylvania Historical Reprints)
Reprinted from *Pennsylvania History*, Quarterly Journal of the Pennsylvania Historical Association, Vol. XIX, No. 2, April, 1952, and No. 3, July, 1952, for the Pennsylvania Historical and Museum Commission

History of Warren County, Pennsylvania
J.S. Schenck
D. Mason and Co., Syracuse, New York, 1887

Kane and the Upper Allegheny
J.E. Henretta
John C. Winston Company, Philadelphia, Pennsylvania, 1929

Kinzua Dam (Seneca Indian Relocation)
Hearings before the Subcommittee on Indian Affairs of the Committee on Interior and Insular Affairs

House of Representatives, Eighty-Eighth Congress
U.S. Government Printing Office, Washington, D.C., 1964

Legends of the Longhouse
Told to Sah-nee-weh, the White Sister
by Jesse J. Cornplanter of the Senecas
J. B. Lippincott Company, 1938

Measuring America—How an Untamed Wilderness Shaped the United States and Fulfilled the Promise of Democracy
Andro Linklater
Walker & Company, 2002

A Nineteenth-Century Journal of a Visit to the Indians of New York
Proceedings of the The American Philosophical Society, Vol. 100, No. 6, December, 1956
Mearle H. Deardorff and George S. Snyderman

Parker on the Iroquois
Iroquois Uses of Maize and Other Food Plants. The Code of Handsome Lake, the Seneca Prophet. The Constitution of the Five Nations.
Arthur C. Parker
Syracuse University Press, 1968

Pen Pictures of Early Western Pennsylvania
Edited by John W. Harpster
University of Pittsburgh Press, 1938

Pennsylvania's Last Indian School
Ernest C. Miller
Pennsylvania History, Quarterly Journal of the Pennsylvania Historical Association, Vol. XXV, No. 2, April, 1958

Pine Knots and Bark Peelers
The Story of Five Generations of Lumbermen
W. Reginald Wheeler, 1960

Pioneer History of Northwestern Pennsylvania
McKnight, W.J., 1905

Report on Indians Taxed and not Taxed in the United States (except Alaska) at the Eleventh Census: 1890
Extra Census Bulletin
Department of the Interior Census Office
Washington, D.C.
Government Printing Office, 1894

Seneca Indians Who Will Be Affected by the Kinzua Dam Reservoir
United States Department of the Interior, Bureau of Indian Affairs
Missouri River Basin Investigation Project
Billings, Montana
Report No. 175, March, 1963

Stillwater: a Novel
William F. Weld
Simon and Schuster, 2002

A Time for Action
The Allegheny Reservoir and Warren County
A report of the Warren County Planning Commission, July 1, 1962

A Traveler's Guide to Historic Western Pennsylvania
Lois Mulkearn and Edwin V. Pugh
University of Pittsburgh Press, 1954

Zeisberger's Allegheny River Indian Towns: 1767-1770
Merle. H. Deardorff, Warren County Historical Society
Reprinted from *PENNSYLVANIA ARCHAEOLOGIST*, Vol. XVI, No. 1

Historical Notebooks
Joseph H. Wick, 1939–1969
Warren County Historical Society

INDEX

978-0-595-38116-6
0-595-38116-2

CPSIA information can be obtained at www.ICGtesting.com
Printed in the USA
BVOW071518220312

285841BV00001B/171/A